ALEX DRAKOS NOTHING LEFT TO LOSE

D1530486

MALLORY MONROE

AUSTIN BROOK PUBLISHING

This novel is a work of fiction. All characters are fictitious. Any similarities to anyone living or dead are completely accidental. The specific mention of known places or venues are not meant to be exact replicas of those places, but are purposely embellished or imagined for the story's sake. The cover art is depicted by models and are not the actual characters.

ALEX DRAKOS SERIES

IN ORDER:

ALEX DRAKOS 1:

HIS FORBIDDEN LOVE

ALEX DRAKOS 2:

HIS SCANDALOUS FAMILY

ALEX DRAKOS 3:

WHAT THEY DID FOR LOVE

ALEX DRAKOS 4:

HIS DANGEROUS AFFAIR

ALEX DRAKOS 5:

A REUNION, A WEDDING, A SCANDAL

ALEX DRAKOS 6:

FOR MY LOVER

ALEX DRAKOS 7:

BRANDING HER AGAIN

ALEX DRAKOS 8*:*

I'LL STAND BY YOU

ALEXT DRAKOS 9:

NOTHING LEFT TO LOSE

VISIT

www.mallorymonroebooks.com

OR

www.austinbrookpublishing.com

for more information on all titles.

TABLE OF CONTENTS

PROLOGUE

It nearly flipped when it made the turn, but Alex Drakos easily corrected and floored it again. Nobody was stopping him now. His aim was straight ahead and he aimed to keep it straight. His entire muscular body was tense and tight as he gripped the steering wheel as he drove. His large blue eyes were so focused on getting where he was going that even the sirens didn't register with him. He was just getting there. Or getting away. He couldn't tell which.

He wanted to phone Kari when the chase intensified. He wanted to phone and tell her that he loved her and that he loved Jordan and that he adored their precious baby, too. But he knew he wouldn't wake her. Because when he left, she was fast asleep. He smiled thinking about how sound a sleeper she was. "Not even a hurricane," he used to say. "Not even a Cat 5 hurricane would wake you up." How did he expect a ringing phone to do the trick?

Karena, he thought, as he looked through his rearview mirror and saw that more cops had joined the chase. Eight was his count. Eight police cars chasing one man. But the man they were chasing was driving a Lamborghini, and he shifted gears again and left them all in the dust. Karena was the love of his life, and Jordan too. And the baby? God help him. How could he do this to them? But it had to be done. He shifted gears again, as he fought back tears. It had to be done!

And he gripped that steering wheel again and focused even more intensely. He saw the roadblock ahead. In the middle of the Tallahatchie bridge was a roadblock. Ten police cars across, with no choke points for any squeezing through, and at least another ten deep. All bright lights flashing in front of him as if it was a ticker-tape parade greeting a hero. But only the parade was on one side. *Their* side. They were finally going to lock up the big man and throw away the key. They intended to stop Alex Drakos. By hook or by crook, they were going to get him this time. By hook or by crook, it was his reckoning day.

But Alex's eyes were big as Kennedy fifty-cent coins as he stared into those lights. As he drove closer and closer to those beautiful lights. And as he drove closer, that was when he saw their guns. All assault rifles. All locked and loaded and aimed straight for his head. This was ending today. On some backwater bridge in some backwater town. They were ready to become legends. Ready to tell their kids and grandkids how they ended it all for a man that always seemed untouchable. They were prime for the fight.

Alex was pumped too. And as soon as he was within range of their kill shot, he didn't slow down. He sped up. He put his feet on the gas, flooring it again, and accelerated to such an extent that the men with the guns became the fearful ones. Some began firing at Alex's car anyway, but most of them dived for their lives as the car was speeding so close to them that they could see the dust off the headlights.

But suddenly, instead of going straight for those cops that had crossed county line after county line to stop him, Alex violently turned his steering wheel with such a hard left that it caused his car to swerve away from all of those sirens and guns and bloodthirsty police officers and end up on two wheels. He turned so hard and so suddenly that his lambo went airborne so high above that bridge that he didn't even hit the rail as he sailed over the bridge and floated in midair. He floated like a plane. The cops, who were no longer fearful now, were firing their assault rifles at that car-plane. Firing as if they aimed to take out his float.

But he had no float. He wasn't driving a

plane, but a car with no floatation device whatsoever. And he began sailing straight down. Dropping like a rock all the way down into that dark, swampy river that was tossing and turning and stormy that morning. As if it wanted to be a legend too.

And then there was silence. That eerie kind of silence that was the darkness before the deeper dark. But the silence broke when Alex and the front end of his car slammed into that river with the loudest splash anybody on the top of that bridge was ever going to hear ever again. And that hungry, anxious, restless river took Alex and his vehicle all the way under.

The cops jumped into their vehicles, with their sirens still blaring, and raced down from that bridge like determined soldiers in battle. The splash below became gurgling, bubbling water, and those bubbles was the sign of yet another roadkill in an unforgiving river that had no lanes.

By the time the cops were down and out

of their cars at the river's edge, there was nothing to see there.

No car. No man. No getting out of there alive.

And they felt satisfied. Some of them even high-fived. Some of them laughed off their dive on the bridge when they thought he was coming straight for them. But still others simply nodded their heads. He didn't get away with it. Finally, they thought, the mighty man had met his well-deserved end.

The great Alex Drakos, one notified their chief, was no more.

CHAPTER ONE

Five Weeks Earlier

The Apple Valley County Fair was in full swing by the time Alex and his family got out of the SUV. Like the rest of the attendees, they all were dressed casually too, mostly in shorts and t-shirts, although Alex and Oz were the oddballs. Alex wore jeans and a tucked-in peach-colored polo shirt instead of shorts and a t-shirt. And although Oz wore shorts and a t-shirt alright, he also wore a vest with his outfit, had his hair in a ponytail, had that big hat on his head, and had one of his fat cigars between his teeth. There was no smoking on fairgrounds, but they always seemed to let Oz and his wonderful, outsized personality get away with murder.

And when he saw the big crowd, and the rides, and the cotton candy, and all the fun and

13

games, that was exactly how he felt. Like all bets were off. He grinned that big, white grin of his that the city called an institution, and he took his pregnant wife by the hand. "Come on, Glo," he said happily. "Let's turn this mother out!"

"Don't you dare, Oz!" Alex yelled after him as he got the diaper bag out of the SUV. "Nobody wants to deal with that."

"Glo's still pregnant, Oz," Kari yelled after him too. "She can't ride on all those rides this time!"

"Don't worry," Oz said. "I got this! Oh and congrats, Kari. You deserve it!"

"I haven't even won it yet."

Oz laughed. Everybody knew Kari was an odds-on favorite to win the Fair Queen award this time around. "Now that's funny," he said.

"Just be careful, boy!" Kari said to him.

"He will," Gloria reassured her, and they took off. They were like two kids in a candy store. They couldn't wait for the fun to begin.

Kari shook her head. "You'll be bailing

his ass out later today," she said to Alex.

Alex put the diaper bag across his shoulder. "Not me," he said. "He wants to act a fool, let him. But he'll be bailing his own ass out."

"They won't let him, and you know it," said Kari. "He's has too many offenses. It's either he's released on your recognizance, or he stays in jail until he goes to trial. And you and me both know you'll never let him rot in jail."

"Don't even try that," said Alex. "Your ass won't let him rot in jail either."

"I know," Kari said, shaking her head. "I am such a hypocrite!"

Alex laughed. That was what he loved about Kari: her honesty. He leaned over and kissed her on the lips. "But you're *my* hypocrite," he said.

"But Mom's right, Dad," said their teenage son Jordan. "You'll be right there with your checkbook as soon as they call you. And Uncle Oz knows it. It's baked in the cake."

"The recipe's changed," said Alex. "He'll find out."

"Sure, buddy," said Jordan, not buying it for a second. Then he saw his best friend. "Matty's here. Ma, Dad, Matty's here. See you guys later!" And Jordan took off too.

"It never ceases to amaze me that every single year when this Fair comes around," Kari said, "everybody in this town acts like they're a kid again. Everybody! Except us." She looked at Alex. "What's wrong with us?"

Alex laughed. "Me? Everything. You? Absolutely nothing."

Kari smiled. "Liar," she said, and Alex laughed again.

And then she and Alex, arm-in-arm, with baby Angela asleep in her pouch, headed into the Fair. They were in a good place in their relationship, but Kari could sense a storm brewing. Because Alex had to go on yet another one of those long-ass business trips. A trip that almost always generated negative press overseas about him with some woman. And he was leaving tonight. "How long this time?" she asked him.

"It depends on the negotiations," Alex said.

"But you can give me a ballpark figure, Al. Come on."

"A couple weeks. Probably longer."

Kari never understood that. "But why is it always so long?" she asked. "Why are there always pushbacks and people leaving the table and why is it always prolonged like that?"

"The nature of the beast, honey. I'm asking them to merge with my corporation, and I'll be in charge. It's a tall ask."

"But necessary?" Kari asked.

"If we expect to stay afloat it is. I've been putting Band-aids on this leak too long. We've got to get out of this hole."

"I know," Kari said. "I just wish you didn't have to stay gone so long."

Kari waited for him to ask her to come

with him if it bothered her that much. But he never asked. One time, when she asked, he said she'd be a distraction. Another time, when she asked, he said she'd be bored because his every waking hour would be devoted to negotiations. She stopped asking.

"Mrs. Drakos! Mrs. Drakos!" It was Palmer Rigsby, the head of the County Fair Commission, hurrying over to them. "You're just in time. The ceremony's about to get started. Come with me!"

Kari kissed little Angela as she slept in Alex's pouch, and then she kissed Alex. "Wish me luck," she said.

"You're a shoo-in, Mrs. D.," said Palmer. "I have that on good authority personally!"

Kari had been hearing that all along, but she wasn't laying any bets. People could say anything in public. But voting was in secret. She'd have to see it to believe it.

Alex, too, saw the doubt in her eyes. He placed his arm around her waist and leaned his mouth to her ear. "Stop looking like that. Just stay positive. Go with the flow. You'll be okay."

But Kari hated putting herself out like that, where she was paraded on some stage to wait and see if she was voted the town's favorite whatever. The last time she did it, she didn't win when they all thought she was going to win. But the commission had nominated her. It was supposed to be an honor just to be nominated. And it was during the annual Fair, an event no citizen missed. She had to show up.

But she was more cynical about why she was nominated. The commission claimed it was because of the jobs she helped create in the community, and all of her charitable work. But people were always nominating her for one thing or another, as if they needed the wife of their most prominent citizen to elevate whatever cause they were trumpeting. And it helped that she added color to the always all-white stages too. But she just didn't like that kind of parade and declined, almost every time, to participate.

But this was the town's beloved annual Fair. This was different.

"If I lose," she whispered to Alex, "it's all your fault."

Alex laughed and, as she walked away, he slapped her on her nice, tight ass.

She glanced back at him with a smile on her face. But after she had disappeared in the thick of the crowd with Palmer Rigsby, Alex's own smile eased. He was exuding confidence about her victory, too, because he knew she could use a win. But he also knew racism was alive and well in Apple Valley. And although he'd been given many assurances that the vote was Karena's to lose, he had his doubts too.

When the loudspeaker said that the Fair Queen voting results were about to be announced, he made his way over to the big stage they had set up. Faye and Benny Church, along with Lucinda Mayes, their oldest friends in Apple Valley, were already waiting. So were Oz and Gloria, and Jordan and Matty, to Alex's surprise.

"See?" said Oz to Alex. "We know how to behave."

"Nobody said Gloria didn't," Alex said, and Jordan and Matty laughed.

Oz, who never took himself too seriously, tipped his hat and grinned.

"Nervous?" Benny asked Alex as Faye and Lucinda doted on little Angela as she slept in Alex's pouch.

Alex nodded. "Always," he responded to his good friend and lawyer.

Benny laughed. "At least the commission nominated her. Faye's a local mortgage broker. She's done a lot for this community. Lucinda too. But they never even get a mention. That commission, in my view, has too much power. They nominate the candidates and they vote on who they think should win. That's a lot of power invested in one body."

"All I know," said Faye, "is that Kari better win. None of that also-ran junk. She deserves to win."

"She will," said Oz. "They say she's got it in the bag."

"I don't believe that for a second," Faye said.

Alex looked at her. "Why would you say that?" he asked her. Because she was sounding like Kari. Was it a woman thing? Was it a black woman thing?

"Just call me cynical about these folks around here," Faye explained. "They talk a good talk, but when they cast those private ballots, nope. I don't see it."

"Me neither, to tell you the truth," said Lucinda, who, like Alex, was white. "They just want diversity, and Kari's the safest choice. Cause Faye and a few other of these people of color in this town will give their asses an earful, and they know it."

Faye laughed and she and Lucinda high-fived. "You got that right!" Faye said.

And then the contestants were paraded

up on stage, a big crowd surrounded the stage, and the winner was announced.

"The fifty-first annual Queen of the Fair is our very own," Palmer said as he opened the envelope for the first time. But then he paused as if he was surprised.

Oh, Lord, thought Alex.

"And the winner is," Palmer said again, regrouping, "Trish Landersome."

The audience applauded, with some cheering happily.

Alex's heart dropped.

"Ain't this some bull?" asked Faye.

But if Kari was disappointed, the audience would never know it. She was smiling and clapping and playing the game as good as it could be played. But Alex saw her eyes. And inwardly they were shooting darts. Her last time playing along, was what he saw in her eyes. She was done. And he was too.

Palmer, still surprised himself, placed the beautiful crown on the head of beautiful Trish

Landersome and paraded her around the stage to the sound of some local tune called *The Queen of the Fair* that was being played over the stereo system. Kari and all of the contestants kept smiling and clapping as Trish was escorted up to the queen's throne, a massive golden chair they had placed at the top of nearly thirty steps high. And then she sat down.

And then the clapping stopped as the drum roll began. "Ladies and gentlemen," Palmer said, "I present to you your queen!"

The clapping and cheering resumed, although Alex nor anybody in his party were clapping at all. They weren't about to go along after so many assurances from the voting committee members themselves. He, instead, was staring at those very committee members. See if they ever get another dime from him for any of their pet projects, he thought. Alex knew it wasn't right, but when it came to Kari, he could be a very vengeful man.

And as the other contestants were escorted off the stage, the big chair began to turn on the turntable so that Trish could wave to everybody on the fairgrounds. But just as Kari stepped down off of that stage, she heard the sound of something breaking. And just as she turned to look back, she saw that massive chair spin wildly around, causing the crowd to scream, and then it dropped through the opening like a malfunctioned ride falling to the ground.

The crowd screamed and gasped in horror as the men, including Oz, Jordan, and Benny ran to Trish's aid. Alex, instead, hurried over to Kari and grabbed her by the arm. His security detail, that had blended in the crowd, suddenly surrounded him and Kari.

"You saw that?" Kari asked Alex and her friends. "Did you see that?"

"We saw it!" Faye said as she and Lucinda ran to see if Trish was alright too.

But Alex saw something else. He saw

that Kari was supposed to be the winner. He saw that every conversation in this town about the Fair Queen award centered on Kari winning. And then the throne malfunctioned? The chair Kari was supposed to be in malfunctioned?

He started looking around, and was prepared to pull out his loaded Glock to defend his family if he had to. "Let's get you out of here," he said to Kari, pulling her against him and Angela.

"But I want to make sure Trish is okay," Kari was saying. She felt, as a contestant, that it was her civic duty.

But Alex felt a different duty. "Fuck Trish!" he said in that harsh tone he could use whenever he felt his family was in danger. And their baby girl was with them too? His heart was pounding. "Let's get you out of here!"

"What about Jordan?" Kari asked as Alex began hurrying her toward the SUV.

"Oz won't let anything happen to Jordan," Alex said as they and their bodyguards hurried away from the crowd.

But when he got Kari into the SUV, and he gave her their daughter and her pouch and diaper bag, he pulled his Glock from the back of his pants, ordered security to stay with his wife and daughter, and ran back to the accident scene. And when he ran beneath the stage, his number one objective was to get Jordan.

When Jordan saw his father, he broke away from Matty and ran to him. "She's dead, Daddy," he said, nervously pushing his glasses up on his face. "Miss Trish is dead!"

Alex nodded because he saw it too. Trish Landersome was indeed dead: she had been crushed by the violent fall. And her husband and mother were with her body, wailing in pain.

But Oz walked over to Alex. Both of them were looking less at the unfortunate victim, and more at the wiring attached to that malfunctioned chair.

"You see what I see?" Oz asked Alex.

Alex saw it. It wasn't obvious to see, but they knew the signs. Those wires had been purposely seared off to make it look as though they burned up in the fall. But they knew the difference. It was no accident.

"Come on, Jordan," Alex said to his adopted son. "Let's go."

Jordan never objected when his father was getting him out of rough spots. And seeing Miss Trish mangled the way she was qualified as a rough spot. He said goodbye to his best friend Matty, and he, along with Gloria and Oz, too, went with Alex.

Alex kept looking around. But everybody looked suspicious to him at that point. So he just kept walking, his arm around Jordan's waist, his heart aching because he knew who could have been in that chair instead of Trish. Because he knew, once again, his family was facing danger because of his ass.

When they all piled into the SUV, and drove away, with their security detail driving behind them, nobody knew what to make of it. But Alex knew what he had to do.

"I'll postpone my trip," he said, as he pulled out his cell phone.

But Kari understood the stakes. "Alex, you can't," she said.

"Yes, I can."

"But why?"

"What do you mean why? Everybody expected you to win. It was the talk of the town. It was a foregone conclusion. Whoever seared off those wires expected you to sit in that seat, not Trish Landersome. They were targeting you. And you expect me to just leave town?"

"But we have a problem, brother," said Oz. "They'll only negotiate with you, and that took months for us to get them to do even that. If those negotiations are tabled, they may not get back on track for another year."

"If ever," said Kari. "You know how that works, Alex. You have to go. We'll be okay. Oz will blanket us. Won't you, Oz?"

Oz nodded. "You know I will."

But it was Jordan who asked the pertinent question. "But who would want to target Ma?" he asked.

Jordan was growing up fast. Too fast, Alex and Kari both knew. But they had no choice. They couldn't sugarcoat their children's experiences. They had to know what being a part of Alex's world could sometimes entail.

"Everybody loves Ma," Jordan continued. "I just don't see how somebody would do something like that to her. Who would want to target Ma?" he asked again.

Alex exhaled, and then he frowned. "I don't know, son," he said with pain in his voice. But what Alex didn't say was that he was willing to bet his corporation that whoever was behind it, the reason had everything to do with him.

But what in the world, he also wondered, could that reason be?

CHAPTER TWO

But Kari and Oz were right. There was no way that Alex could miss that particular business trip and expect to get his corporation back on sound footing. Later that night, his plane flew him out of Florida to France.

And while in France, he was calling home many times every single day. Especially during the first two weeks. The family was okay, was always the response he got, and Oz consistently had no news. Their people weren't able to find out who did it, or why they did it, or any news whatsoever. And the commission didn't help.

Their haphazard investigation had concluded that the chair apparatus malfunctioned and poor Trish Landersome's death was ruled a tragic accident. Oz tried to explain why they were wrong, but they didn't want to hear it. They would not entertain any alternative versions. But Alex and Oz knew better.

And as the weeks came and went, and as the negotiations sputtered along, with many tense times causing the talks to fall off the rails to a degree where Alex was forced to compromise a little more to keep it all on track.

But it kept sputtering along. The least disagreement meant a delay of sometimes hours, and there were also complete walkaways that lasted a full day.

On one such day, Alex and his security detail made it back to his hotel in Provence, France early that evening, only to find an old friend and flame, Judette Demaris, sitting in the lobby.

"Alexio!" she said with her cheerful

French accent as she rose to her feet.

Almost as tall as Alex, she was easy to spot. Alex smiled and walked over to her. She was a breath of fresh air. "Hello, Judy. It's been a long time," he said as they embraced. "What brings you to Provence? Are you still living in Paris?"

"But of course. Where else is there to live?"

Alex laughed. He was drained and tense. He could use a good laugh. "Sit down," he said as he unbuttoned his suit coat and they both sat back down in the luxurious lobby. Alex's bodyguards remained nearby.

"I know you are a busy man these days," Judette said.

"And how do you know that?" Alex asked.

"I read the papers. They say the negotiations are, how do you say in America? High stakes? Would you disagree?"

Alex shook his head. "No. I would not."

"That is why I will be brief. I do not want

to take up any more of your time than I must. Unless you are as hungry as I am, and you want to take me to dinner."

But Alex was too curious about why she dropped by his hotel at all. "What is it that you came to discuss?" he asked her.

"Not to discuss," said Judette, "but to warn you."

That caught Alex's immediate attention. Because he immediately thought about Kari. Did it have something to do with what happened at the Fair? "Warn me about what?" he asked her.

"You must be careful, darling. Very careful. Because they have something very powerful on you, and they will not hesitate to use it if you are not careful."

It sounded like a riddle to Alex. "Who are they," he asked her, "and what is it that they have on me that's supposedly so powerful, as you call it?"

"I cannot say who, and I cannot say why.

I was told to warn you."

Alex frowned. "But warn me of what?"

"What I just said."

"But all you said was for me to be careful. What's that supposed to mean? What am I being careful about? The negotiations?" He was negotiating with FiberCarp, one of France's premier industrial giants. A corporation that size and of that stature would not get in the mud like that. Or would they?

But Judette was still cagey. "I do not know what it is about," she said. "They did not tell me what it is about."

"But at least tell me who they are," Alex implored.

"I do not know that either. I was only told, by phone, to warn you."

"Some stranger phones you, and you do exactly what they say? You expect me to believe that?"

Judette didn't have to think about it. "Yes," she said unequivocally.

Alex stared at her. "What do they have on you that would make you approach me like this?" he asked her.

For the first time, Judette seemed less self-assured. Even frightened. "Nobody's past is perfect. Certainly not mine. They know things I would rather they not know." Then she looked him dead in the eyes. "They told me to warn you."

"And if I told them to take their warning and shove it up their asses?" Alex asked.

"I will not relay that message. Because they are serious, Alexio. They had things on me that nobody should have had."

But Alex stood up. His whole life was a chess game. His whole life was a series of moves. "You tell them I'm not interested. If they want to warn me, tell them to do it to my face."

Judette stood up too. "They also told me," she said, "that if what they have on you were to ever come to light, that your family, that your wife, would leave you."

Alex was stunned to hear those words.

"That is the nature of the information that they have," Judette said. "You see, my darling," she added, "it is not the usual thing *atall*."

No, Alex thought, it was not. Because he was a man with a past too. A very ugly, unflattering past.

Then Judette smiled and placed her arm around his arm. "Let's just go to dinner, Alexio," she said. "Let's just eat!"

It was typical Judette. Nothing was ever that serious to her.

But Alex had responsibilities she would never dream of having. Everything was serious to him.

CHAPTER THREE

Kari woke up, the next morning, to a series of phone calls. One after the other one. First from Lucinda, who was blunt. "Another trip overseas for Alex. Another bimbo eruption for you."

Kari hadn't even opened her eyes as she turned onto her back in bed. "What are you talking about, Lou?" She was so sleepy still that her voice was a little more than a whisper.

"The news out of France," said Lucinda. "At least according to Mary in the Morning."

Mary in the Morning was a part of a local AM news program where she spilled the tea, as she called it, on Apple Valley's very own rich and famous. But Kari couldn't help it. She'd been running around like a mad woman for the past week trying to get the hotel and casino ready for state inspections that were scheduled for the following week. She fell asleep on Lucinda's call.

But then Faye Church called. And other friends called. And by the time she had gotten up and showered and dressed for work, the local press was calling her to comment too. She wasn't about to give any comments to the press for them to turn around and misinterpret. She hung up in their faces.

But even Gloria called her too, asking if she'd watched the morning news hour. "No," Kari said as she grabbed her briefcase and made her way downstairs in the penthouse. "But I heard the news."

Alex, according to Mary, was spotted in Provence, France with some fashion designer when he was telling Kari that he was in high stakes negotiations that was consuming every second of his time and talent. It was nothing but the usual bullshit, she assured Gloria and the rest of her friends, too, and they all seemed satisfied with her *nothing-to-see-here* response. But inwardly Kari was getting concerned. He'd been gone for three whole weeks. A lot could go wrong in three weeks.

And Alex's calls had been getting more infrequent.

Until that morning, after the news broke locally, and he phoned her.

She was pulled out of a meeting of all department heads when the call came in. She couldn't even remember where she'd left her cell phone, that was how busy it was that morning. He had to contact her secretary to find out where she was, something she knew he hated doing. When she hurried to her office and took the call, he was in a mood.

"Where were you?" he asked before she could sit behind her desk.

"Meeting with the department heads," she said over her desk phone. "The inspectors will be here in just over a week, remember? I want no issues."

"I don't know why you won't let Bud handle that." Bud was The Drakos hotel's general manager. "He's paid to do all the worrying for you."

"I'm not worrying," Kari said. "I'm just trying to make sure we have our hotel in order. They were harsh on us last time. I want no unforced errors this time."

Alex didn't respond to that, but Kari knew his silence meant he wasn't buying what she was selling. He was going to believe she worked too hard no matter what she said. So she stopped saying it. Besides, they were talking about everything except what they needed to be talking about.

Until, like always, Kari had to break the ice. "When are you coming back?" she asked him.

"Soon."

"You said that last week, Alex. And the week before that."

"What do you want me to say? That I'll be back tomorrow? Will that make you feel better?"

Kari frowned. "Don't talk to me like that. Negotiations may be going bad, but that's not my fault."

Alex exhaled. "You're right. It's not your fault."

"But negotiations are going bad?"

"Getting there. It's dicey right now."

"On a scale of one to ten, how important is this merger?"

"A hundred," said Alex.

"Damn, Al. And what does it mean if it falls through?"

"It can't fall through. That's what it means."

It was Kari's time to exhale. Although The Drakos hotel and casino were on solid ground, she knew The Drakos Corporation, a separate entity, had major equity issues. They needed a merger to stay afloat he told her, and they needed a record-breaking one. All of the efforts from the past to shore up the business had ultimately failed. No more piecemeals, Alex had decided. He was going for broke.

And it looked like that was exactly what he was getting.

"Oz found out anything new?" Alex asked.

He was talking about that incident at the Fair, but Kari shook her head. "Still no leads at all. No video footage. No informants coming to tell what they know. Nothing. It's like nobody knows anything."

"Damn," said Alex. And then he exhaled.

"Maybe the commission's right, Alex," Kari said. "Maybe it was just a terrible accident."

Alex knew better than that. "Yeah, maybe," he said, but even Kari could tell he was only saying that to alleviate any fears she might still have.

But then the purpose of his call came into focus just as Jordan walked into Kari's office. The call was already on Speaker, and Kari kept it that way. She and Jordan grew up together. She was an unwed fifteen-year-old when she had him. She kept few secrets from him. Besides, he was a smart young man with an ambitious future. She was certain he heard about those press reports already anyway.

"It's a bunch of bullshit, Karena," Alex finally said to her.

"I know," Kari said so quickly that she felt as if she was on autopilot when it came to Alex and those bimbo eruptions she'd had to deal with the entirety of their marriage.

"It's nothing for you to be worrying about," he added.

Kari leaned back in her chair. "Who is she?" she asked. She didn't look at Jordan, but she could feel his intense stare.

"A friend," said Alex. "An old friend."

"Very cozy pictures the paparazzi took of the two of you." She only saw a couple photos. Nothing in and of themselves telling. But the press was good at misinterpreting.

"It's a free-for-all here in Europe, I told you that," Alex said. "Two old friends have dinner together and they turn it into a love affair."

Had Kari been petty, she would have pointed out how many days he'd told her he didn't call her because his every waking moment was devoted to negotiations. But yet in still he had time to have dinner with some friend?

But Kari wasn't petty. She knew that was one of the things Alex loved about her. She was ride or die come hell or high water. And he knew it. But lately she wondered if he was taking advantage of that knowledge.

"I'd better get back to the negotiation table," Alex said. "I didn't know it was even a story until my assistant mentioned it to me. Thought I'd call and make sure you were okay."

"Yep." Kari wasn't okay. She missed him, she was still a little worried about that Fair incident, and Oz had been treating her and Jordan like prisoners at the Drakos. They could hardly go anywhere!

"I'll try to give you a call tonight," Alex

said. "And make Bud take up some of that load. He should be the one meeting with the department heads, not you."

"Uh-hun." Kari wasn't about to agree to that. For Bud, The Drakos was a job. For her, it was her life. And if Alex's corporation failed, it just might be their only source of revenue. She wasn't delegating shit to Bud.

"Jordan and Angie okay?" Alex asked her.

"Yes, they're fine," said Kari. "Jordan's right here."

"Tell him I said hello and you have a good day," Alex said.

"You too," said Kari. And the call ended.

She hesitated, still wondering if she was letting Alex off too easy, before she looked at Jordan. By the look on his face, she knew she was.

"It's bullshit, Jordan," she said to her beloved son.

"But what if it's not, Ma? You saw how

46

snappy he was before he went on that trip, and now this? And all he has to say to you is that it's not true and you believe him every time."

"And every time it's proven to be just what he said it was."

"Not every time," Jordan said. "Most times you don't know if it's true or not."

Kari didn't respond to that. Because he wasn't lying. "What do you want?" she asked him.

Then sensitive Jordan continued to speak his truth. "For you and Dad to get back to your happy place," he said to his mother.

Kari looked at him and smiled the smile of a woman who knew it was high time too. "We will, son," she said. "We will."

CHAPTER FOUR

"This is going to be a nice surprise."

"Let's hope Alex thinks so."

Oz looked at Kari through his rearview mirror. "Why wouldn't he think so? His wife and son meeting him at the airport after he's been gone an entire month? He's going to be ecstatic! He'll probably pull you onto his plane and make out with you before we leave that airfield. I know my brother. He's going to be thrilled to see you guys again. He'll be thrilled to see Glo again. He may even be glad to see me too." Oz said it with a grin.

"I wouldn't go *that* far," Jordan said, and Oz laughed out loud as he turned another corner and then was on a straight glide to the private airfield.

He glanced over at his wife Gloria, who was plump and pregnant and seated on the front passenger seat beside him, but she wasn't speaking to him that week so she refused his offered hand. He looked through the rearview at Kari and Jordan and sleeping baby Angela. Jordan was his usual upbeat self, but Kari was subdued like Glo. And although he understood Glo's reason - he'd fucked up again, he didn't understand Kari's. "Everything okay, sis?" he asked her.

Kari smiled a tired smile. "I'm good," she said the way a selfless woman who didn't want to worry her kid would say. Because Jordan was always in tune with his mother's feelings. He honed that skill when it was just the two of them struggling to make ends meet in a town that had no welcome mats for them. He even looked over at his mother when she responded to Oz. He looked over at her as if he knew what was bothering her better than anybody on earth.

Oz didn't know for certain, but he'd bet

good money that the source of her concern was the same source it always was: that brother of his. "What has he done this time?" Oz asked her. He was bold like that.

Gloria, stunned, looked at him. "What is that your business?" she asked him.

But it was instructive to Oz that Glo knew exactly who the *he* was that he was talking about. He looked through his rearview again.

"He didn't do anything," Kari said when it was clear Oz wasn't going to take silence, nor Gloria's admonishment, for an answer.

But Jordan finished what he knew his mother was thinking. The man who had adopted him and made him his own meant the world to him and his mother. When something was wrong with Alex, something was wrong with all of them. "He'd been snappy on the phone lately," Jordan said. "He won't let us go anywhere or do anything."

"You know it's because of what happened at that Fair," Oz said.

"But that was a month ago. The committee said it was a malfunction. They said the heating element burned those strings. They said they weren't cut like you and Dad believes."

"They can say whatever they want," said Oz, "but we saw what we saw. Those wires were intentionally burned."

"But if he's so worried about us," said Jordan, "he should have come home long before now. He's always snappy on the phone with Ma. They're always arguing."

This surprised Oz. Gloria too. But then again, they'd had their own share of problems and hadn't been asking about any phone conversations. Gloria asked about that woman in Provence, but when Kari said it was nothing, that was as far as it went.

But that was why, when Kari said she was going to meet Alex's plane, Oz and Glo were thrilled to go too. They'd all missed Alex. He was their anchor. The man they all went to with their problems. The man who was even more a voice of reason than Kari was in the family. They had no idea anything about him had changed. "Any reason for it?" Oz asked Jordan. "Other than he's worried about you guys?"

"None he's telling us."

"When did it all start?"

Jordan looked at his mother. "Every time he calls pretty much. Right, Ma?"

Kari nodded. "Something like that."

"But what was different about him?" Oz was still taking his eyes off the road and looking through the rearview every chance he got.

"He seemed bothered by every little thing," Jordan said. "Ma told him he needed to cool it. But they'd get into it and it'll only get worse. He was better at the Fair. But then that incident happened and so much for that. The last time he and Ma talked on the phone was like a week ago, and it didn't go so well."

Kari looked out at the Friday evening traffic when Jordan spoke those words.

But now, as Oz drove the SUV up to the airfield and they saw that Alex's plane had already landed, Kari braced herself. For some reason, she felt antsy and uneasy as if something wasn't right. But she didn't realize what it was that had her feeling that way until the airstairs of the plane came down and Alex began walking down those steps. And they saw the woman.

CHAPTER FIVE

"There he is!" Oz said happily as they drove onto the tarmac.

But a limo was already waiting at the foot of the plane's stairs. And when a woman got out of that limo, Oz automatically slowed down, and then came to a complete stop. He glanced at Kari through the rearview. What was his brother up to? This was Oz's kind of bullshit, not Alex's!

But they all sat in that SUV staring at Alex. He wore one of his designer suits, a Hugo Boss if Kari had to guess from where she sat, and a pair of dark sunglasses. Looking gorgeous as usual, she thought. What woman wouldn't want a man who looked like Alex? But that realization didn't make her feel any less uneasy.

And the way he and the woman were going at it seemed less like some kind of business meeting and more like a lovers' quarrel. It got so heated that the woman and Alex both were pointing at each other.

"What's that about?" Jordan asked as he was staring intensely too.

"Business, I'm sure," Oz said, although he didn't believe it himself. But he wanted to alleviate some of the fear he heard in Jordan's voice. He knew Jordan admired Alex just as much as Oz admired him. He knew that anytime your hero fell short, it made you feel as if you'd failed too.

And then, to make matters worse, the woman turned to get back into the limo, but Alex grabbed her by the arm and turned her back around to face him. As if he was determined to continue the argument.

And they continued arguing like business associates, or quarreling like lovers. It depended on how you looked at it. But in that SUV, even Gloria and young Jordan viewed it as a lover's spat too. It had all the earmarks. Why get all that hot and bothered over some business associate?

But they all were mostly just worried about Kari.

Kari kept her opinions to herself. She stared at her husband unable to be so quick to judge him the way they could. Alex and Jordan and baby Angela were her world. How was she going to be able to handle anything upsetting their family unit? Because that woman Alex was jawing with was no bimbo eruption. She was a woman willing to go toe to toe with a tycoon known for not allowing anybody to go toe to toe with him. Except for Kari. She was always the exception. Until now.

When the woman finally snatched away from Alex's grasp, she got into the limousine and the limousine drove off heading toward Oz's SUV. It was only then did Alex look in their direction. When he recognized Oz's SUV, he exhaled, as if he was still getting over that confrontation, and then began heading toward the SUV. The limo kept on driving away from the airfield altogether.

"Why don't we drive over to him," Gloria said to Oz.

"He can walk," Jordan responded to her.

Kari looked at Jordan, Gloria turned around looking at him, too, and Oz looked at him through the rearview. Yep, Oz thought. Jordan was feeling the sting of the fall of his hero.

And Oz did as Jordan suggested, and stayed put.

Alex walked slowly toward Oz's vehicle as the other SUV there to pick him up followed behind him. Until he told them otherwise, his driver and bodyguard inside that SUV weren't leaving his presence.

But as Alex approached Oz's SUV, he realized his kid brother wasn't alone on this surprise pickup. He saw Gloria on the front seat, but Kari and Jordan and Angie were seated on the middle row. And his heart dropped. Did they see that argument? Did they see him with that woman? What more, he wondered, did they have to put up with him? Or did they take it for what it most certainly was not: just another disagreement between two business associates?

Jordan got out of his seat and moved to the third row of the SUV when Alex opened the back door on Kari's side.

Kari moved over to let him in, and Alex could feel the tension as if it were a blade on his neck. But even with that tension, he missed his wife and children so much that he placed his arm around Kari, said hello to her, and then kissed her on the lips. He could feel her almost turn her face away from him as their lips met, but something about his kiss kept her there. Because he certainly couldn't break away from her if his life depended on it. He even wrapped her in both of his arms and kissed her passionately, as if they were in their bedroom, and not in his brother's ride.

Kari, too, could not break away from that man. It had been a month. A long, agonizing month, and she'd missed him in her bed. Every morning waking up alone was no fun for her. And it was hard too. Whenever she saw a good-looking man, she would get horny for Alex. If she was getting that way, how was he managing when, unlike her, he was constantly surrounded by great looking women? It was just stressful for her! But Alex's masterfully passionate kiss could not be denied.

When they finally stopped kissing, Oz looked at his brother. "Are you two kids finished?" he asked them.

Alex smiled. "Hello to you, too." Then he glanced at Gloria. "Hello, Gloria."

"Hello, Mr. Drakos."

Oz rolled his eyes. Why was this woman still calling her brother-in-law *Mister*?

But Gloria couldn't help it. Alex Drakos reminded her of her own father, the boss of all mob bosses Mick Sinatra, and she could never be casual with a man like that.

Alex kept his arm around Kari but leaned

59

beyond her to sleeping Angela in her car seat, and he kissed her too. And then he looked back at Jordan. "How are you, son?" he asked him. "Been taking care of your mother for me?"

Jordan wanted to get flip with Alex. *For you? No. For her? Yes.* But he wasn't that kind of kid. He pushed his glasses up on his face and nodded his head. "Yes, sir," he said. But he said nothing else. Which was not like Jordan. He loved Alex as much as Kari did. He was pissed with how Alex was treating his mother and he was tired of hiding it.

And Oz, seeing all of it, drove away.

Kari looked at Alex as the SUV began to move, and as the SUV already on site to pick Alex up began following them. She needed to know. She couldn't wait another second when it seemed obvious to her that Alex would rather not discuss it at all. "Who was that?" she asked him.

Alex shook his head. "Nobody," he said.

But Kari continued looking at him. He

had to know her better than that. "Who was that?" she asked him again.

And this time he gave her an answer. Not a satisfactory answer, but an answer. "Just business," he said as if that said it all. And when she kept staring at him, he looked at her. Only his look wasn't inquisitive like Kari's. His look was chilling, as if he were making it clear to her with that look alone that he was not going to discuss it further in front of the boy. And not in front of Oz and Gloria, either, for that matter.

Kari knew she could have argued the point. They'd had the equivalent of knockdown-drag-out arguments in their marriage before. She was good at arguing the point. But she could feel Jordan's big eyes, beneath those glasses he wore, staring at her. She decided to wait.

And they rode in silence the rest of the way to The Drakos where all of them lived. And Alex squeezed Kari tighter against him as they rode home.

But nothing had changed. Her mind was still on that woman who had been at the airfield with Alex. And that other woman in France the press made hay about a week ago. And her concerns would not be swept under a rug this time. That rug was beginning to wear thin with Kari. They were going to get into it.

Alex's mind was on both women, too, and that major-ass problem they represented. He knew if Kari ever got wind of that situation, she just might leave him forever. And his ass would be right back where he started from: a lonely man with nothing but his wealth and his selfish lovers to live for. Until Kari and Jordan came into his life. And they were trying to ruin what he had without even telling him what it was about? They were trying to turn his own family against him and expect no retribution from him? They had the wrong one if that was their thinking.

But Alex thinking about it still sent shivers up his spine. He talked a good game, and he was infamous for presenting an unflappable exterior. But inwardly he was as scared as a child. Inwardly he was terrified.

Because he still didn't know what all the threats of blackmail were really about. How the hell could he fight back when he didn't know what he was fighting about? He had to send out a message, he thought. A message that would be loud and clear.

Both women claimed his family would leave him when it came to light. But the woman at the airfield, Elsie, was a particularly nasty bitch that he should have taken out a long time ago. She worked for his father once, and was in on an attempt on Alex's life that went sideways. The nerve she had showing up now! But she had the same story as Judette had. They made her do it and she didn't know who they were and she didn't know why they were doing it to Alex. She was there to warn him. And although he knew nobody in their right mind would threaten to expose him unless they had something major to expose, he wasn't about to become anybody's sitting duck.

As he held Kari closer to him still, he made a decision too. He decided that it was now time for him to send a warning of his own. A warning that would shake that tree, and shake up whatever plans they had, so that he could see the fallout himself.

CHAPTER SIX

They had only just arrived at The Drakos Hotel and Casino in Apple Valley, Florida when Alex's phone was ringing and Bud Bainbridge, the hotel's GM, was waiting to pull him aside to fill him in on what all happened during his monthlong absence. Kari could have handled that job herself, since she was the actual boss in charge in Alex's absence, but she let Bud have his say. She and Bud didn't always see eye-to-eye. He didn't appreciate the way she ran things most of the time, and he was going to give Alex an earful. But that was his deal. He had a right to have his say.

While Alex moved aside to answer his phone and to talk with Bud, and while Gloria headed off to the restaurant she owned in town, and while Jordan headed over to his friend Matty's house to hang out on a Friday evening, Kari took the baby to The Drakos daycare inside the hotel where her two nannies were waiting to take care of her, and then she headed to her own office.

She didn't realize Oz was behind her until her secretary, who was about to leave for the evening, said hello to him.

"Are you stalking me?" Kari asked him.

"Something like that," Oz said with a grin and followed her into her office, closing the door behind them.

"What is it?" Kari asked him as she stood in the middle of her office.

"I wanted to make sure you were okay."

Kari smiled, but even Oz could see it was a tight smile. "I'll be alright, Oz," she said and rubbed his muscular arm. "Thank you for caring."

"Alex has to do better."

"Yes, he does." But then she stared at him. "And so do you."

Oz looked at her as if he had no clue. "What do you mean? Gloria been talking to you?"

"She didn't have to talk. I know when she's upset with your ass. And she's upset with your ass. And pregnant. You need to do better too."

Oz placed his hands on his hips and nodded his head, his long hair flapping as he nodded. "Correct," he said.

And then there was silence. Kari wasn't about to discuss her marriage issues with Oz. And Oz knew it. "Just wanted to check on you, that's all. When you're doing good, the whole family's doing good. At least that's how I see it."

Kari smiled. "Thanks, Oz. But I'm alright."

He nodded again. "Good. But I'd better get back to the casino before Alex wanna kick my ass. And you know what that means."

"That you'll get an ass-kicking?" Kari asked.

Oz laughed that booming laugh Kari loved. "He wish!"

But as he turned to leave, Kari couldn't help herself. "Oz?" she asked.

"Yup?" He turned back around.

Kari hesitated, and then just asked it. "Am I crazy to believe I'm the only woman Alex be with?"

Oz's heart dropped. What was wrong with these Drakos men? "Alexio loves you more than any living creature on the face of this earth, Karena."

"That's not what I asked you. Am I insane to think I'm the only woman Alex be with?"

Oz exhaled. The fact that he could not say no outright said it all to Kari. "I'll be honest with you," he said. "When Alex first hooked up with you? Yes, I thought any woman was out of her mind if she thought my big brother was going to be her one and only. But with you, he's been different."

"You still haven't answered my question. Am I crazy to think I'm the only woman Alex be with?"

Oz exhaled again. "Let's hope not," was the best he could say to her. And then he and Kari stared at each other with knowing eyes. "I've got to get back to work," he said, and was about to leave the office. But then Alex walked in.

"Get to the casino, Odysseus," Alex ordered. "There's a drunk looking for a brawl. Go handle it."

"A brawl tonight?" Kari asked as she and Oz began heading for the exit. "We have inspections tomorrow! There's no way we're having any brawls tonight."

But Alex grabbed her arm. "Oz will handle it. I need you to come upstairs with me."

Oz knew what that meant. Kari knew it too. And she could have told him hell no. Not until you tell me who that woman was. And more about what happened in Provence. But she knew when to pick her battles. While Oz hurried to contain the violence in the casino, she went upstairs with Alex.

NOTHING LEFT TO LOSE

CHAPTER SEVEN

The woman from the airfield sat in the back of the limo still angry with Alex. As her driver sped through the streets of Pensacola, Florida on its way to the bed and breakfast where she was staying, her cell phone began ringing. When she looked at the Caller ID, she hesitated before answering. But she knew she had no choice in the matter. Nobody did.

She answered the call. "Yes?"

"How did it go?"

"Like I told you it was going to go. He's pissed."

"He would not be upset had you handled it correctly."

"I handled it correctly, what are you talking about? I did everything you told me to do. I don't know what else you expect from me. We're talking about Alex Drakos!"

"I know who that fucker is. You don't

70

have to tell me."

The woman sighed. "What do we do next?"

"Keep the pressure on. He's going to wish he'd listened to you."

"Well, he didn't. Not at all. He thinks he still rules the world. He's about to realize--" She frowned and looked at what she thought she saw in her peripheral vision. And when she turned her head, she realized it was true. She saw it coming. She saw it coming!

"*God no*," she said with adject terror in her voice as her hand went limp and the phone nearly dropped.

"What are you talking about, Elsie?" the man on the other end of that phone was asking her. "*God no*, what? What is it, Elsie? What is it?"

But it was too late for her to respond. The tractor trailer came barreling toward that limo like an out-of-control locomotive and slammed right into the side where Elsie sat, shattering the glass, violently tearing through the door, and knocking not only her phone from her hand, but her entire body from where it sat to the other side of the limo.

When the limo stopped flipping, the lifelessness inside was only tempered by the eerie sound of Elsie's name still coming from the man's voice on her discarded cell phone.

CHAPTER EIGHT

He closed and locked their bedroom door and began kissing her passionately again as he pulled her into his arms. Kari didn't resist. How could she? It had been one long, lonely month. And Alex wasted no time. He was kissing his wife as if he was a desperate man. He was walking her toward the bed and was removing her clothes as if he'd never had a woman like her in years.

By the time they made it to the bed, her upper body was naked and she was feeling the heat too. And he swiftly removed his suit coat, untied his tie, and lifted his tie and his shirt and t-shirt off of his upper body in one fluid motion. He tossed them aside. And then he laid her on the bed, with his body on top of hers, and began sucking her breasts.

Kari ran her fingers through his hair as he sucked her. Nobody did her better. And when he moved down further, between her legs, she stretched her body out across that bed and gave him full access. It had been so long since she was with Alex that she nearly came in his mouth. That was how magnificent it felt. And Alex nearly came, too, just by doing her. Which made him well aware of the risk of giving her only part of what he had to give. It was branding time again. It was time for him to remind her who she belonged to again. He abruptly stopped and stood up.

He removed his shoes, his pants, and his briefs, revealing his long, hard erection, as he stared at how red and wet Kari's breasts and vagina had become from his mouth alone. If he had given out that much heat already, he could only imagine what he was about to put on her.

He got back on top of her, and wrapped her into his arms, and then he eased his penis deep inside of her with one hard thrust. A thrust so electrifying that it caused Kari to let out a scream that was so primal, and so erotic that it made Alex almost cum right then and there.

But he knew how to hold on. And he held on. And they eased into a long, sweet, highly-sensual coupling that had both of them groaning.

For nearly half an hour they did it together, looking at each other, kissing each other, speaking sweet nothings to each other. Until, in a break from their usual way, it was Alex, not Kari, who came first. He tried to hold on longer. He tried to make it last forever. But Kari's body was so tight and his penis was so hard that he had to have his release. He poured into her.

And Kari wrapped him even tighter in her arms and allowed him to fill her up. Until her will power broke, too, and she was cumming right along with him.

They came for several minutes. It wasn't the usual out and done and that was it. It had been a long time coming. And their bodies were responding to that absence. Kari used to think that she'd know if Alex had been with another woman when he came home from one of his trips just by the way he responded to her body. But he always responded to her body as if he was sex starved. She gave up speculating long ago.

They continued to cum, and hold onto each other, until their slow-rock became an even slower-rock, and they eventually ran out of juice.

And then they just laid there, still holding each other, with Alex still deep inside of Kari.

When he finally pulled out of her and rolled off of her, they laid on their backs for several more minutes, both attempting to regulate their breathing again and both attempting to find the words to say. Because there were words that needed to be said. *Who was that woman in Provence? Who was that woman at the airfield? What the hell was going on*?!

Kari was the first to turn toward Alex as

she turned onto her side. Alex remained on his back still breathing heavier than she was. But she waited patiently. And then he finally looked at her.

"The woman at the airport was just somebody I used to know, Karena," he said to her. "Somebody from my days back in Greece."

"Was she there to discuss business?" she asked him. "Or was it about more than that?"

Alex was not going to lie to her. "More," he said.

Kari felt a pang of sadness pierce through her body. "What did she want?"

"Nothing. Old shit. Don't worry about it."

Kari understood Alex still had female friends who used to be more involved in his life before he married her. She understood that. But that didn't make it easier to take. "And the woman in Provence?" she asked. "The woman in France?"

"I told you a week ago she was an old

friend."

"Another one?"

Alex didn't like the sound of that. "Yes. Another one."

"With or without benefits?"

"There was a time she had benefits, yes," he admitted. "But we're just friends now."

Kari exhaled. "I always tell people it's nothing but bullshit when I hear about you and some woman whenever you're on these business trips. But now I'm beginning to wonder if the bullshit's on me."

Alex looked at her. "You know me better than that, Karena." But when he saw that the sadness remained in her eyes, he pulled her into his arms, a frown of deep concern on his face. "I'll never hurt you," he said, and Kari leaned into his embrace.

But as he thought about Elsie at the airport, and Judette in France, and how both of them warned him that his family would leave him if the so-called truth came out, he had another thought. He wouldn't hurt Kari. He'd already made that plain to her. But he wasn't about to let anybody else hurt her either. Nobody was tearing them apart.

That was why he had given the order to take out Elsie for that very reason. That was his shot across whatever bow was trying to stir shit up. He once ran his old man's crime syndicate before he left it all behind and became a businessman in America. He could stoop down to that level with the best of them. He could stoop even lower than they would ever think about stooping. And they had to understand that.

CHAPTER NINE

The next morning Alex was stuck in his office attempting to clear his desk of a pile of monthlong paperwork that required his review and signature, while at the same time studying the market trends up on the television screen in his office when his personal assistant walked in. But a call came in from Matthew Scribner, his CFO from his corporate headquarters in New York, before he could respond to her. He answered his desk phone quickly. "Good morning."

"I take it you're watching Bloomberg," Scribner said.

"I see we slipped a few more this morning," Alex responded. "That's three weeks in a row. Should I start getting worried?"

"Not at all, Boss. Nothing to worry about. I got our experts to look behind the numbers just to be certain, and they all agreed it's just a course correction. GM and ALCOA are taking hits too. There's no volatility yet, and we'll shore it up to make sure we have no wild swings. We're good."

"Sir?" His assistant was shoving an envelope into his face. Alex looked at the envelope and then looked at his assistant. She didn't play games. Something was up. "Talk to you later," he said into the phone and hung up. "What is it?" he asked his assistant.

"This was just delivered, sir. It's marked urgent," she said as Alex took the envelope from her hand.

Alex could feel that photos were inside the envelope, which immediately made him suspicious. "Who brought this package to my office?" he asked her.

"One of the local couriers. He said a man paid him triple to hurry it over. And yes, I asked for a description or a name. He couldn't give me either."

"Couldn't or wouldn't?" Alex asked.

His assistant nodded. "Right, sir," she said.

Alex exhaled. "That'll be all," he said, and she gladly left what she felt was a firing squad. And Alex opened the envelope.

The photos weren't racy at all, as he had suspected they would have been. But that was what made them immediately chilling to Alex. They were photographs of Kari at the outdoor market checking out fruits and vegetables. Only the photos were date-stamped for today. Within minutes ago, as if they were taken, downloaded, and then handed to the waiting courier. Alex jumped from his chair and began hurrying out of his office and calling the security chief assigned to Kari's detail.

"Where's my wife?" he asked anxiously as he ran out of his office and up to the elevator.

"She's here at the marketplace, sir."

Alex swiped his card and jumped on his private elevator. "You have your eyeballs on her right now?"

"Yes, sir. Right now, sir."

"How close?"

"I have two of our men within ten feet of her, sir."

"Get closer. Break your cover if you have to. Blanket her!"

"Yes, sir," the chief said. "Right away, sir."

Alex got off of the elevator, and he ran toward the exit. His heart was pounding. Had his shot across the bow with Elsie put his own wife in danger?!

CHAPTER TEN

What those photos didn't show was that Jordan, carrying his baby sister in a pouch in front of him, was also at that outdoor marketplace with his mother. He had been further over, well out of frame of those photos, but he, Kari, and the baby were side by side now, both checking out the organic foods stands. Security had been tightened by two men Kari and Jordan had never seen before because they were meant to be clandestine, and therefore paid them no attention.

But they mainly weren't as attentive to what was going on around them because they were in an intense conversation. Jordan was admitting he was having doubts.

"Doubts about what?" Kari asked him.

"About Dad."

Kari stopped in her tracks and looked at her beloved son. He was filling out now into a very handsome, very intelligent young man whom she and Alex both had the highest expectations for. "What kind of doubts would you have about your father?"

"About The Drakos Corporation. He wants me to take over when he steps down."

"*If* he ever steps down, yes," said Kari. "But in the meantime, we expect you to go to college, get your MBA, and then join him at the corporation. Why would you not want that all of a sudden?"

"It's not that I don't want it," Jordan said.

"Then what is it, boy?" Kari asked.

"I want to get married someday, and have a happy family."

Kari frowned. "What's that supposed to mean?"

"Dad's out of town a lot." Jordan said this and then looked over at his mother. As much as Alex and Kari tried to put on a united front in public, Jordan knew there was still trouble brewing in their marriage.

"What does his being out of town have to do with you getting married and having a happy family?" Kari asked.

"I don't want to neglect my wife the way . . ." Jordan stopped himself.

But Kari knew exactly what he meant. "The way you think Daddy neglects me?" she asked him.

Jordan looked at her and nodded. "Yes, ma'am."

Kari exhaled and continued to look at the organic produce. "Alex doesn't neglect me,

Jordan."

"He's out of town a lot," Jordan said.

"He runs a Fortune 500 company. What do you expect?"

"But that's why I don't know if I want to run a Fortune 500 company. I don't want to sacrifice my family for the company's success."

Kari looked at him. "Come on, Jordan. Just stop. You know Alex is not sacrificing us for the sake of his company. You know that."

"Not us," said Jordan. "But you."

"How is he sacrificing me, boy? What are you talking about?"

Jordan hesitated.

"Just say it!"

"The kids at school says Dad cheats on you."

"They're lying."

"But how do you know he's not cheating, Ma?"

"How the hell do they know he is?" Kari shot back. "You're going to listen to some

87

school kids about your own father? A man you know would never hurt us?"

Then Kari exhaled. She couldn't pretend that she didn't understand where all the talk was coming from. Alex and his past were always good gossip fodder. "He's not that kind of man, Jordan," she finally said.

"Every man's that kind of man," Jordan said.

That surprised her. That didn't even sound like Jordan. "Says who?" she asked him.

"Uncle Oz," he responded.

Kari rolled her eyes. "Child please. Listen to Oz if you want. Glo isn't always running back home to her own daddy for nothing. Oz's ideas of how a man is supposed to act, especially a married man, leaves a lot to be desired, okay?"

"I know that."

"And don't you forget that."

"I'm just saying I don't know how I'll be able to balance a strong family life with working for Dad. Uncle Oz knows how to cut loose and have some fun in his life, and he's a successful businessman too. Daddy don't do that. That's all I'm saying."

Kari couldn't argue with that point. Alex was a lot of great, wonderful things, but fun-loving wasn't one of those things. And they continued shopping.

In a blue sedan across the street, a man was taking even more photographs of Kari. Only he wasn't using a traditional camera, or even his cell phone because he knew security was always around the wife of Alex Drakos. What he used, instead, was a camera embedded in the tint of his car's window. He held the remote that aimed and took the photos. There was no way he could be detected.

Until he heard what sounded like a pop-a-lock from his passenger side door and, just as he was looking to see what the noise was, Alex Drakos was getting into his car. His heart stopped.

There was no way, he thought, he could be detected! But Alex detected him as soon as he got on scene. From the non-tinted back window of that car, he could see the man staring over at Kari. And he never stopped looking at her during the entire time Alex was walking up on that car with a slim jim in his hand. He easily popped that lock and got onto the front passenger seat beside the man before the man knew what was going on.

"I wasn't doing anything!" the man immediately confessed as his eyes showed his fear.

"Who said you were doing something?" Alex asked him.

Alex could see the man attempting to reach down for a gun he apparently kept in a side pocket inside that car. And Alex didn't hesitate. He quickly leaned over, grabbed the man's arm, put it behind him with such force and so violently that the arm broke.

The man tried to scream out in pain, but

Alex covered his mouth. "You going to fuck around with me, or are you going to tell me the truth?"

He pulled even harder on that already broken arm. The man tried to scream again. He looked at Alex nodding his head.

"The truth?" Alex asked.

The man nodded anxiously again as sweat was already beginning to break out on his face. He was in tremendous pain.

Alex removed his hand from the man's mouth. The man was now panting. His screams were over.

Alex released his broken arm, which only made it hurt even worse as he tried to move it around to the front to cradle it.

"Who do you work for?"

"I work for myself."

"Doing what?"

The man hesitated. Alex reached for his other arm and slung it behind him.

"Okay!" the man cried. "Please! Okay!"

He'd heard how Alex Drakos was not the one to play with, but seeing him in action made that statement the understatement of the century.

"I'm just a photographer, Mr. Drakos," the man said. "I was hired to take undercover photos of your wife and upload them to different throwaway phones that gets thrown away every time after I send in photos."

"Who hired you?" asked Alex.

"He said they'd kill me if I ever said his name."

Alex pulled the man's second arm back as far as he could and broke that arm too. He covered the man's mouth again as the man couldn't help but scream out in unbearable pain.

But he had to bear it as Alex had to have that name. "You think they'll kill you if you don't give me that name? Think about what I'll do to you if you don't give me that name." Then he yanked on that broken arm again.

The man's screams were muffled screams beneath Alex's massive hand. "Are you ready to tell me who?"

The photographer anxiously nodded.

"Or do I need to break a kneecap too?" Alex asked.

The photographer anxiously shook his head.

Alex removed his hand from his mouth. But he kept his hand on that man's second broken arm.

And he didn't hesitate this time. "Lekas," he said. "Marty Lekas."

Alex frowned. "Marty Lekas?" He knew him. They'd done business in the past before. Lots of business.

Alex yanked the man's arm again, causing him to clench his teeth to fight back the excruciating pain. "If you're lying to be, I'll be back. You understand that?"

"I'm not lying. Marty Lekas hired me. I was the photographer at his daughter's wedding."

"You won't be taking any more pictures

any time soon," Alex said. "But that's what your ass gets for messing with my family. Now you leave them the hell alone. You hear me?"

The man's head was leaned back against his head rest. "I hear you. I've never heard another man like I hear you," he confessed.

And Alex finally let go of the man's second broken arm. And then he got out of the car, buttoned his suit coat, and walked across the street toward his family.

Jordan saw him coming before Kari did, and he was shocked beyond measure. "Dad?" he said out loud.

Kari looked at Jordan, and then looked where he was looking. When she saw Alex coming from across the street, looking like the sexiest man alive to Kari, she could hardly believe it too. She just knew he'd be swamped in paperwork his first day back at the office. Which made her immediately suspicious.

But he, instead, was smiling when he approached them. "Hey there," he said.

Jordan was smiling too. It was a pleasant surprise. "What are you doing here?" he asked him.

"You three have a market day and don't invite me?" Alex asked.

"We didn't think you'd come," Jordan said honestly.

His honesty was always welcomed by Alex, but it cut him a little too. "Sometimes I have the ability to surprise you," he said.

Jordan laughed. "Yes, you do," he said.

Alex ruffled his hair as he took his baby girl from Jordan's arms. Angela was wide awake and smiling when she saw her father's face. "Hey, baby," Alex said to her. "How are you, my little angel?"

Then Alex looked at Kari. "Hey," he said as he bounced the baby in his arms.

"Hey," Kari said.

"It's hot out here," said Alex. "Go get us a couple beers, Jordan."

Jordan looked at his father. "Dad, they

aren't going to sell me beer."

Alex forgot just that fast that Jordan was still a teenager. He always seemed so far beyond his years. "Get me a coke then," he said.

"Yes, sir. You want one too, Ma?"

"I'm good," Kari said, still staring at Alex. And Jordan went inside the store area of the outdoor marketplace.

Alex looked at Kari as the two men that had been blanketing her began to pull back. Nobody was going to protect Alex Drakos's wife, they knew, better than Alex Drakos himself. "Nice day for shopping," he said.

But Kari knew Alex too well. "There's a threat?" she asked him.

He continued to bounce his baby. "Why would you think that?"

"You at the marketplace this time of day? With all that work on your desk? What else am I supposed to think?"

"That I wanted to spend some time with

my family."

"Is there a threat, Alex?"

Alex nodded. Kari was not the one to play with either. "Yes," he said. "There was a small one."

Kari was concerned. Their baby and son were there. "What is it?"

"There was a creep taking pictures of you. That's all. But I handled it."

"I hate when guys do that," Kari said. "I was at the gym inside The Drakos and I saw a guy snapping photos of one of our female customers."

"What did you do?"

"I cussed his ass out and threw him out," said Kari. "What do you think?"

Alex laughed. "I'm surprised he wasn't taking pictures of you."

"Yeah, right. Me and my ponytail. Sure, Alex."

Alex was always taken aback at how little regard Kari gave to her beauty. Because there was no one more beautiful on this earth to him.

But he had a more pressing problem. And his name was Marty Lekas. "Anyway," he said, "I've got to go to Chicago in a couple hours."

Kari was shocked. "Alex, you just got back!"

"Just a day trip. A quick turnaround. But some business I have to take care of."

"It can't wait for at least a few days?"

Alex wished. "No," he said. Not even a few hours, he wanted to say. "But I'll be back in time for dinner."

Kari doubted that, but what could she do? The man ran a major corporation. Things came up all the time. At least he promised to return tonight.

She wanted to know more, but Jordan came back up with a coke for his father, and one for himself. And then the baby started crying as if she wasn't crazy about Alex going away again either.

CHAPTER ELEVEN

Later that evening, before going home for dinner, Kari dropped by Mars, a local bar to have a drink with her two closest friends: Faye Church and Lucinda Mayes.

"She finally decides to drop in," said Lucinda as Kari took a seat beside her. The bar was loud, with televisions on all over the big space. Some on sports channels. Some on news channels. One with an old *Bonanza* rerun. "After all this time, she finally decides to show up."

"And not a moment too soon because our asses were about to leave," said Faye.

"Cut me some slack, ladies" said Kari. "I

had inspections this afternoon."

"Oh, right," said Lucinda. Although Faye was a real estate broker who had an office, it was Lucinda who was in retail too. She used to own a diner she sold to Gloria. She understood all about state inspections. "How did it go?"

"Good, thank God," Kari said as the bartender came over.

"Welcome to Mars, Mrs. Drakos. What can I get you, ma'am?"

Did everybody know her name around Apple Valley? It felt weird sometimes when people she'd never seen before in her life knew her name. "A martini, thanks."

"Coming right up," the bartender said and went to make the drink.

Lucinda tossed her short, blonde hair back as she took a sip of her already made drink. She was the only white woman in the threesome, and she was also the only one drinking like it was all about the liquor rather than just getting together with friends. "No major infractions?" she asked.

"None, thank God. There were a couple hiccups in the casino, and I could have kicked Oz's ass for letting that go unnoticed, but it was minor overall. We passed."

Lucinda raised her glass in an imaginary cheer. "Good for you," she said.

"What I don't get," said Faye, "is why would they do inspections on a Saturday of all days?"

"To try and trip us up," said Kari. "Our busiest day of the week and they want to inspect? Those bastards know what they're doing."

"Here, here," Lucinda said with another imaginary toast. Kari and Faye glanced at each other. Lucinda had been hitting the bottle pretty hard lately.

"Take it easy, Lou," Kari said. "We don't have a designated driver."

Lucinda smiled. "No worries. I'm like a fish. I can just suck this stuff up like it's milk. It does nothing to me."

"Ha!" It was Faye's one-syllable laugh. "Believe that shit if you want to." And she took another sip.

But then Kari heard Alex's name and all three ladies looked up at one of the televisions. The one carrying local news.

"I said it right, folks," said the anchorwoman. "Billionaire industrialist Alex Drakos is in hot water with the ladies once again. This time a former model by the name of Bridgette Venew is set to hold a press conference at the rival Hollingsworth Hotel in Pensacola Monday afternoon. According to her publicist, she will uncover what is being called Mr. Drakos's unspeakable sins. Since it concerns our most prominent citizen, Action News will carry that press conference Live."

Lucinda, shocked, put down her drink and looked at Kari. Faye was already looking at Kari. Even the bartender, Kari noticed, gave her a look of pity as he sat her glass down in front of her. Kari hated those looks. But she took a sip from her drink.

"Kare?" Faye said.

But Kari waved her off. "There's nothing to it," she said. "Just a --"

"We know, we know," said Lucinda. Then she and Faye looked at each other. "Just a bunch of bullshit," they said in unison. And then Lucinda looked at her. "We know."

"That's what you always say," said Faye.

Kari looked at both women. "What do you mean?"

"We mean that's what you always say," Faye said again. "You always say that same shit when Alex is accused by any woman of anything."

Kari stared at them. And a thought suddenly occurred to her. "Am I that girl?" she asked them.

Faye was especially concerned for her best friend. "Yes," she said.

"Think about it, Kare," said Lucinda. "It's

so many incidences. *Too many*."

"You want us to tell you the truth," said Faye. "And that's the truth of it. Lou's not lying. It's a lot, Kare."

"I had a cheating husband," said Lucinda. "I know what it looks like. Sometimes everybody else can see it before you can."

But Kari began to grab back up her phone and keys.

"Come on, Kari," said Faye. "You don't have to leave."

"I'll talk to you guys later," she said, got up from the bar, and left.

Lucinda and Faye watched her leave, and then they looked at each other. "Bullshit my ass," said Lucinda. And then she burped.

CHAPTER TWELVE

Marty Lekas was sprawled out on the massage table on his stomach when the masseuse came into the private room at the private Chicago spa. "I want it straight down the middle this time, honey," he said. "Ass and all. I've been the proverbial tight ass all week for some reason."

The masseuse turned out to be Alex, and Alex pulled out a switch blade and carefully began to cut, just above the surface, Marty's back. "Down the middle like this, honey?" he asked him.

As soon as Marty first felt that blade on his back and then, when he heard that familiar voice, he rolled off of the table and grabbed the gun he had lying atop his discarded clothes.

But Alex was faster than the husky man ever could be and he grabbed Marty's hand that contained the gun, ran him across the room and slammed his back and his gun-toting hand against the wall, knocking the gun from that hand. "What the fuck are you up to?" Alex angrily asked him. "What are you trying to do to my family?"

"It's not me, Alexio. You know it's not me! I wouldn't do anything to your family."

"Who is it then?" Alex asked.

"I don't know who. They called and told

me to find a way to let you know they not only have you in their crosshairs, but your wife too."

"Who are they?"

"I told you I don't know! I don't know the people. I've never met them before in my life."

"Then how do you know it's a they?"

"Because the guy said so in our phone conversations. He said it's a group of them and I had to do what they told me to do."

It sounded just like Judette's story, and Elsie's to Alex. But Marty Lekas too? "Your ass ain't weak," Alex said. "Why would you do whatever they told you to do?"

"Because my ass dirty too!" Marty said. "And they got some of that dirt. Some serious dirt. I had to do what they wanted. But I wasn't gonna hurt anybody. That's why I didn't call in any mob guys. That's why I used a real photographer and not some mob guy."

Alex exhaled. "Did he say why he was targeting me and my wife?"

Marty shook his head. "He didn't tell me

nothing. Just that you were in their crosshairs, and they wanted to show that it was nothing to put your wife in their crosshairs too. I tried to tell them what you were capable of, and that they were barking up the wrong tree, but he didn't wanna hear it. They saw what happened to Elsie. Even I knew it was you sending their asses a message, but he still didn't want to hear it. He wanted you to know they had your wife in their crosshairs too. No matter what. They said something about a county Fair."

Alex's heart dropped. Now it was confirmed that it wasn't an accident that killed Trish Landersome, and that it was all tied in together. But who were they tying it in, and why on earth were they after him? And now Kari too?

But he believed every word Marty said. Because he knew him just that well. But he still punched his lights out for not coming to him when he was threatened, and for hiring that photographer to stalk his wife, but it wasn't a death penalty offense. He released him.

But when Alex got back outside and into his SUV, it all still felt as if he was spinning his wheels. And then, as his driver drove him back toward the airport, his bodyguard, who sat up front with the driver, turned and looked at him. "We got a problem, Boss," he said.

"What problem?" Alex asked.

"Bridgette ass supposed to be holding a press conference Monday afternoon."

Alex frowned. "Bridgette?"

"That's what the media's saying. They say she's going to meet the press on Monday."

"To say what?"

"To say you did some serious shit to her. Some unspeakable sins, as they called it. I checked with every media source we have. But nobody knows what exactly those sins are yet."

Alex couldn't believe it. "Did my wife hear about it yet?"

"It was all over the news in Apple Valley," the bodyguard said. "I don't see why she wouldn't have."

It was all Alex needed. He pulled out his cell phone and called Kari's cell. But it went to Voice Mail. She always answered his calls. Unless she left her phone somewhere, or she was pissed with him. He suspected the latter was the reason.

Alex looked at his driver. "Put fire in it," he said.

"Yes, sir, Boss," his driver said, and his slow, scenic drive became a sprint to the airport.

CHAPTER THIRTEEN

The quiet felt loud as they slowly ate dinner. Because Kari wasn't thinking about the food in front of her, and neither was Jordan. And even the normally vivacious Oz was having a hard time with this one too. He kept taking peeps at Kari. Jordan kept taking peeps at her too. But Kari's expression remained expressionless. A press conference on Monday? A woman about to claim horrors at Alex's hand? This was not something Alex was going to b.s. his way out of. Kari was going to see to that.

But it was Jordan who broke the ice. "Where's Gloria?" he asked his uncle.

Oz looked at him. "She's Aunt Gloria to you."

"Come on, Unc. She's not that much older than I am." But Oz continued to look at him. "Where's *Aunt* Gloria?" he finally said.

"She's back in Philly."

Kari looked at Oz.

"She ran home to Daddy again," Oz said. "I told her that shit was getting old."

But Kari continued to stare at him. "What did you do?" she asked him.

Oz hesitated, but he answered honestly. He always did. "I party too much, she claims."

"That's the shit that's getting old," Kari said. "You and that partying."

"I know, I know, okay? We Drakos brothers are in everybody's shit house right now. I get it. But there's two sides to every coin."

"What's the flipside, Unc?" asked Jordan. "That Aunt Gloria should party more too?"

Oz grinned. "Yeah!"

"Un-hun," said Kari. "Be careful what you wish for. You married a very desirable woman. Let her get out there if you want. You may not stay married to her for very long."

Oz's grin slowly dissipated. And he

nodded. "I do miss her desperately," he admitted. "But she's not returning my calls yet."

"What does Mick say about it?" Kari asked.

"What he always says. Hurt his daughter and he'll kick my ass."

Jordan grinned. "What did you tell him, Unc? In his dreams he'll kick your butt?"

Both Kari and Oz exchanged a glance. Jordan apparently had no real idea who Mick Sinatra really was.

"That's what you told him?" Jordan asked.

Oz shook his head. "Not quite," he said.

"Then what did you tell him?"

"I thanked him for hearing me out and ended the call. What the fuck you think I told him? That's Mick the Tick you moron. Have you ever bothered to look him up?"

Jordan laughed. "I was just messing with you. I know you're Mister Tough Guy with everybody except Gloria's dad for some reason.

I guess he's the real tough guy."

"Fuck you, Jordan," Oz said, and Jordan laughed.

But it wasn't long after that that the quietness returned. And they continued to eat their meals in silence.

But as a testament to the level of stress they all were enduring over that news of that upcoming press conference, they all jumped when the front door of the penthouse opened. And when Alex made his way into the dining room, they were no longer pretending to have any interest whatsoever in what was on their plates. They were all staring at Alex.

Alex was staring at Kari. And although her look was almost expressionless to Oz and even to Jordan, Alex knew better than that. Because nobody knew her better than him. He saw the pain in her eyes as soon as he looked at her. And the anger too. He had some serious explaining to do. "Jordan, why don't you finish your dinner in your room?"

Jordan, always an obedient young man, was about to pick up his plate. But Kari stopped him. "No," she said. "He needs to know what's going on too."

Oz looked at Alex. Nobody defied that man. Not even Oz. And he could tell his brother was pissed that Kari had tried to. He even saw Alex's jaw tighten.

"Jordan," Alex said again, "go to your room."

Jordan knew who ultimately wore the pants in their family, and it wasn't his mother. He got his plate and soda and went to his room.

And then Alex sat down in the seat at the table that Jordan had vacated. And he wasted no time. "I'm being blackmailed," he said to Kari and Oz.

They both were surprised, and they sat up straighter in their seats. "Blackmailed?" Kari asked. "By this Bridgette woman?"

"And the woman in Provence, France. And the woman at the airport. Not them

115

personally, but they were sent by the people who are trying to blackmail me."

Oz was shocked. Although he had a happy-go-lucky side to him that seemed to dominate his personality, when it was all on the line there was nobody more serious, or more committed, than Oz. "Who are they?" Oz asked.

"Nobody knows at this point," said Alex. "I've got men checking it out, but nothing so far."

"But what do they have on you like that, brother?" Oz asked Alex.

For Alex, that was the most painful part of all. "I don't know," he said.

But that was a non-answer to Kari. "What do you mean you don't know? What did they say to you?"

"Bridgette said nothing. I haven't heard from that woman in years."

"And the other two?" Kari asked.

Alex exhaled. "They weren't specific either. They were sent to warn me. That was all they had to say."

"Damn," said Oz.

But Kari still wasn't satisfied. "If they weren't specific, then what did they say generally?" she asked him.

Alex couldn't come to grips with what they really said himself. He couldn't verbalize that they said his family would leave him if they knew the truth. "They said it's bad," was as far as he was willing to go.

But Kari continued to stare at him. She knew he was holding back. "Oz?" she asked as she continued to stare at Alex.

"Yes, mother?" Oz responded in his usual playful manner.

"Take your ass home," Kari said in no uncertain terms.

Oz and Gloria lived at The Drakos, too, in an apartment below the penthouse. And like Jordan, he, too, knew who wore the pants in that family. But unlike Jordan, he believed the person who owned the heart owned the power. And he firmly believed that Kari owned more of

Alex's heart than Alex had ever given to any human being that ever existed. Now that was power. Kari, Oz concluded, was the real boss of the family. "Yes, ma'am," he said, got up, and left the penthouse.

Kari was still staring at Alex. "You've been bullshitting me, Alex," she said. "You tell me what those women said to you, and you tell me the truth now."

Alex frowned. "Who the fuck you think you're talking to like that?"

"You!" Kari shouted back at him. "I'm talking to your ass! I defend you, Alex. No matter what shit they throw our way, I defend you. My friends think I'm some misguided female who'll believe anything her man tells her. I'm not that girl. I know I'm not. But I'm sure as hell beginning to sound like that girl every time these fucking bimbo eruptions erupt and all I can say is that it's bullshit. And you're going to disrespect me by not telling me the whole truth? Fuck you!"

Alex already knew Kari was angry. But now it was on full display. She was ready to walk away from that table, and maybe their marriage, too, if he wasn't careful.

He leaned forward. The anguish in his eyes wasn't lost on Kari. "They said," he said to her, "that if you and Jordan found out the truth, you would leave me."

Kari's heart dropped. "But what is the truth?" she asked him.

"I don't know. I swear to you I don't know! I have racked my brain trying to figure out what it could be."

"And?" asked Kari.

Alex leaned back. "In my past," he said, "there are too many things that it could be. I wouldn't know where to begin."

Kari exhaled. She didn't marry a saint. That was all there was to it. She married a badly flawed man who scratched and clawed for everything he got. Who gave it to his enemies ten times worse than they gave it to him. Who never did anybody dirt unless they did it to him. A man, she also knew, with the biggest heart in the world. And he was under siege. Which meant she was under siege too.

She got up from her chair, went over to Alex, and pulled him into her arms. "No matter what comes out," she said to him, "me and Jordan leaving you is off the table."

Alex looked at her with those big, sincere eyes that seemed almost on the verge of tears. Those same eyes that made her fall in love with him when they first met.

But for Alex, it was even deeper than that. Kari was his safe place. She was where he decided to land his heart, and she nurtured it and cared for it ever since. Despite the enormous pain his past actions caused her, she never wavered in her love for him. "I love you, Karena," he said to her with a heart so heavy with emotion that it came out as if it was the hardest thing in the world for him to say. When, in truth, it was the easiest.

"I love you, too, Alex," she responded to him with a serious look on her face. Because their love for each other was never as simple as words. It wasn't romantic. It was tried by fire. It was messy. It was hard.

Before his bright eyes shed any tears, which would have been shocking for Kari to see, he pulled her onto his lap. And then carefully, lovingly, pulled her into his arms.

CHAPTER FOURTEEN

Jordan jumped out of his car and race through the side entrance that led into the lobby.

"Where's my dad?" he asked Bud, the GM, as he ran toward him. "Where's my mom?"

"They're both in your father's office, I think," Bud said. "Are you okay?"

But Jordan didn't have time to respond. He was already running toward his father's private elevator. He swiped his keycard, the doors slid open and he got on, and he leaned against the wall to catch his breath as the elevator hurried him upstairs. When he got to his father's office floor, he hurried off of that elevator and ran across the massive expanse and into his father's suite of offices.

His mother and father were seated on the couch in Alex's office, and the television was turned on. "Has it started yet?" he asked as he looked at the television screen and hurried

122

toward the couch.

"Why aren't you still in school, Jordan?" Kari asked him.

"I wanted to see it," Jordan admitted freely.

"You didn't have to leave school, boy! You could have went to the bathroom and saw it on your cellphone."

"I wanted to see it with you and Dad," Jordan said.

Alex and Kari immediately felt ashamed. Now he was drawn into Alex's lurid past too. But when Alex adopted Jordan, they made sure Jordan understood something most young boys never had to even think about. He was not only taking on the wonderfulness of having a wonderful man like Alex as his father, but Alex's baggage too. Which was a long way from wonderful. Jordan understood that.

As proof, he sat, not beside his mother at a time like this, but beside his father, effectively sandwiching Alex in between Jordan and Kari.

As if they, for a change, was holding him up. Alex placed his arms around both of them, and leaned back on the couch, leaning them back with him. And Alex crossed his legs as they waited for that press conference to begin.

"Did you go and see Angie at the Daycare?" Kari asked him. The daycare was inside The Drakos.

"No, ma'am," Jordan admitted, although he usually went and got his baby sister when he first get home from school. "But I'll get her after this is over."

Kari and Alex glanced at each other. Will it ever be over, they wondered?

And then the TV reporter announced that the woman was about to appear, and all of the commentary ceased as the cameras focused on the podium in the room. But just as the woman was about to show her face, Oz hurried into the office, his long hair loose and flapping around his broad shoulders. "Has it started yet?" he asked them.

But they were all too intensely watching the screen to respond to Oz. Oz sat on the arm of the couch next to Kari.

But when Bridgette Venew finally walked into that hotel conference room in Pensacola and stood at that podium, and the media began flashing camera lights at her as if she were some movie star, Kari, Jordan, and Oz were astounded by her beauty. But Alex was astounded by something far different. He removed his arms from around his wife and son, and leaned forward, his face so deep in concentration that he had a fixed frown on his face.

"I'll be brief," Bridgette said as she unfolded a sheet of paper and began to read from it. "I was twelve years old the first time I had sex with Alex Drakos."

As soon as she said those horrible words, an audible gasp filled the entire conference room and those camera clicks went ballistic. Jordan's mouth flew open, and he quickly looked at his father. Oz looked at Alex too. But Alex and Kari were staring at the screen. Kari leaned forward, too, and became shoulder to shoulder with Alex.

"From that moment on," Bridgette continued, "it never stopped. He'd pass me around to his friends and other members of his family, too. It never stopped."

Oz was shaking his head. "What a pack of lies!" he declared.

"And he passed me around to high up executives in his corporation too," Bridgette continued. "It never stopped. I'm twenty-five years old now, strung out on drugs because of how he fucked up my mind, and the last time I was with him was two weeks ago in Paris."

Even that last line confounded Oz. He looked at Alex again. Jordan did too. But Kari and Alex were still staring at the woman on the screen.

"He told his wife he was there on business," Bridgette continued, "and some of the time that was true. But most of the time that wasn't true. He was going between me and all those other women he had set up in France. He's a sick, perverted, deplorable man who has to be stopped. No telling how many other girls he'd been with. No telling what he's done to so many other innocent women. He's a monster," she said as her voice cracked. "He's a monster!" she yelled. Then she folded her paper, and as reporters shouted questions at her, she left the room.

The anchorman and anchorwoman at the news station began talking about what they'd just heard, but nobody in Alex's office was listening to them. The damage was done. It was all about cleaning up the mess at this point. Because it was a mess.

"It's a pack of lies," Oz said again. But this time it sounded more like a question than a declaration.

But Alex was stoic. So was Kari. And Jordan was still in shock. He didn't know what to believe!

And it all just angered Oz. "What's with you guys?" he asked Alex and Kari as he stood up. "Why aren't you talking? Shouting? Cussing her ass out?"

But Kari looked at Alex. It was an accusation she knew wasn't true with every fiber of her being, but it was also the kind of accusation she couldn't say was bullshit and call it a day. That was for Alex to say and do. "What's going on here?" she asked him.

"That's what I want to know," Alex responded, his eyes still transfixed on the television screen as they still had Bridgette's photograph on that screen.

All of their cell phones began ringing simultaneously and they all began getting notifications of text messages, too, but they ignored it all. And then the door to Alex's office opened. It was his secretary. "Sir?"

Alex finally broke away from his trance and looked at her. "Yes?"

"The lawyers are on conference Line 5."

But Alex couldn't even respond to her. He looked back at the television screen and that photograph that remained staring back at him.

"He'll phone them back," Kari said to his secretary.

"But they said--"

Kari gave her a hard look. What part of he will phone them back did she not understand?

The secretary understood. Kari could be as hard as her husband you rubbed her wrong. "Yes, ma'am," the secretary said and left the office, closing the door behind her.

"I don't get it," said Oz, still confused by their reaction. "Where's the outrage?"

Kari looked at him. "Outrage? For what?"

Jordan was shocked by his mother's question. "For what? For what that lady just said about being twelve and all," he said to her.

"Nobody's getting outraged over that

bullshit," Kari said. "And yes, it's bullshit again." She looked at Alex again. "How do you know this Bridgette Venew?" she asked him.

"That's the thing," Alex said. "That's the thing."

"What's the thing?" Kari asked him.

"I don't."

Everybody looked at Alex. "You don't what?" Kari asked him.

"I don't know her. That's not the Bridgette I know."

"You mean she wouldn't make those allegations of her own free will? You mean she's changed?" Kari asked.

"I mean that's not her." He was still studying that photograph on screen. And then he looked at Kari. "I've never seen that woman before in my life."

They all were floored. "Are you telling us, brother," Oz asked, "that the person who just gave that press conference is an imposter?"

Alex nodded. "That's exactly what I'm

telling you."

But Jordan felt as if they were missing the point. "But what about the fact of her being twelve years old and all of that?" he asked.

Kari and Alex both looked at him. "It's a lie, Jordan," Kari said.

But Jordan was still looking at Alex. He had to hear it from his father. "It's not true, Jordan," Alex made clear. "None of it is true. And the woman who delivered those lies aren't even the woman she's professing to be."

They all could see Jordan inwardly sigh relief. "I knew you wouldn't do anything like that. I just needed to hear it from you."

Alex put an arm around him. "I've done a lot in my past that I'm not proud of," Alex admitted, "but I've never done that. And never will. You hear me, son?"

Jordan nodded. "Yes, sir. But why is she lying like that? And why is she claiming to be this Bridgette Venew when you're saying that's not Bridgette Venew?"

"That's the million dollar question," said Alex.

"In the meantime," said Oz, "you need to get those lawyers asses up in here. If my radar's right, and it usually is, that woman is looking for a big payday, and then she'll retract the story. It's extortion in broad daylight."

But Alex had another thought on his mind. "Come with me, Karena," he said as he stood on his feet and helped Kari to her feet.

"Where are we going?" she asked as she stood up too.

"We're going to the source," he said.

When it still didn't register what he meant, he was blunt. "To Bridgette," he said. "We're going to see Bridgette Venew. The real one." And that was all Kari needed to hear.

"Get Angie," Alex ordered Oz as they began hurrying out of the office, "and keep the press away from Jordan."

"Neither child shall be out of my sight for a second," Oz proclaimed in that sweeping voice he loved to display.

But Jordan wasn't thrilled at all with such a pronouncement. "Help us all," said Jordan. "Not another lock down!"

But Alex and Kari didn't hear him. They had already left the office.

CHAPTER FIFTEEN

It was a back corner booth in a smoke-filled, dark and dingy dive in Brooklyn, New York. The overweight woman seated in the booth wore makeup that appeared to have been put on in the dark, as her bright red lipstick went beyond her thin lips, and her eyeliner went well beyond her eyes. She had a lit cigarette in one hand and a bottle of Heineken's in the other hand.

When she looked up and saw two people standing at her booth, one of which she definitely recognized, her expression didn't change one iota.

"Hello, Bridgette," Alex said.

"Kiss my ass," Bridgette responded.

Kari was surprised by the appearance of the woman Alex called Bridgette, especially in light of the bombshell that called herself Bridgette at the press conference. And she was also surprised by the woman's reaction to Alex, as if what that woman said at that presser had a grain of truth to it.

But Alex was accustomed to Bridgette's nastiness. She'd been that way the whole decade he'd known her. Even when she was a beauty. Even more so after she lost her looks to drugs and alcohol. He motioned for Kari to sit at the booth across from Bridgette. Kari sat and slid over. Alex sat beside his wife.

"Did I invite you and your bitch to sit at my table?" Bridgette asked.

"Watch your mouth," Alex said.

"Make me."

Alex grabbed her wrist and twisted it. "Ouch!" she cried.

"Watch your mouth," he said. "Call me whatever the hell you want. You don't call my wife anything."

"Okay!" Bridgette said with irritation in her voice and Alex released her wrist. She took a long drag on her cigarette, and another sip of her beer.

"How you been doing, Bridge?" Alex asked her.

"I told you to kiss my ass."

"I don't have that kind of time," Alex said. "You got a big ass."

Before Bridgette could catch herself, she broke out into a throaty, smoke-filled-lungs of a laughter. That was the Alex she remembered.

When her laughter died, and it took a minute, she took another sip of her beer, another drag on her cigarette, and then her look turned serious again. "They tried to threaten me," she said. "But they didn't know me like that."

Kari looked at Alex. Was she going to be the one to finally give them some answers?

Alex was hoping too. "Who are they?" he asked Bridgette.

But she ended up giving the same answer everybody else had given to him. "How should I know who?" she said. "They didn't leave their names. They didn't leave any business cards."

"What kind were they?" Alex asked her because he knew she'd understand what he meant.

"Scary guys. Wise guys that go bump in the night." Then she frowned and tapped the ash off her cigarette. "Who the fuck cares?"

"What did they want you to do?" Alex asked. "To lie on me?"

"They wanted me to get lost so they could parade Prissy Mae in front of the cameras and pretend she's me. And for her to lie on you. And boy did she put on a show."

"A show filled with nothing but lies," said Kari.

Bridgette looked at her. "So this is your . . ." She started to say bitch. "Woman," she said instead.

"Watch your mouth," Alex warned her again. "But yes, she's my wife."

"Your *wife*?" Bridgette laughed. "Your

ass got married? Now that's a twist! We all tried to get our hooks in you by any means we could come up with, and this one did the trick? I find that hard to believe."

Alex started to reprimand Bridgette again, but Kari placed her hand on his arm. It didn't matter. They weren't there to convince some drunk that Alex loved her and married her above all the women he could have married because of that love he had for her. They were there to find the truth. And if that meant letting that dog have her day, Kari was willing.

Alex understood what Kari's hand on his arm meant. Get on with it. So he did. "Just tell me what they said to you," he said to Bridgette.

"They said they'd pay me to get lost for a few days."

"Just a few days?" Alex asked.

"That's what they said. I told them okay. They paid me and then they left. And I came right back here. It was the easiest money I ever made."

"And that was it?" Alex asked.

"That was it."

"Why would they want you to disappear only for a few days?" Kari asked.

"And the bitch talks," she said. "My my."

It took everything within Alex not to slap the shit out of Bridgette. But Kari took over. "Why would they want you to disappear for only a few days?" she asked again.

"They didn't tell me none of that, okay Shaniqua? They weren't going into any details with my fat ass. Do you understand what I'm saying to you?"

"How much did they pay you?" Kari, still ignoring her little putdowns, asked her.

"Now that's none of your business," Bridgette said.

"How much did they pay you?" Kari asked again.

Bridgette frowned. "What difference does that make?"

"It'll let us know if they meant business,

or if it was just window dressing."

Kari was well beyond Bridgette's level of thinking. "What's that supposed to mean?" Bridgette asked her.

"How much?" Kari asked yet again.

Bridgette realized she wasn't dealing with some idiot Alex scraped off of the street. He had himself a woman with brains. "Five hundred bucks," she said to Kari.

It was Alex's time to frown. "That's all?" he asked her.

"That's it."

He and Kari both were surprised by such a low number. And why would they only want her to get lost for just a few days? Something wasn't adding up. Or was she even telling them the truth?

Alex exhaled. He was as confused as Kari was. "Where did they get that cockamamie story of abuse?" he asked Bridgette.

Bridgette laughed that throaty laugh again. "From out of thin air," she proudly proclaimed. "It wasn't from my childhood. I must be one of the few women in America who never been abused a day in her life. Yet that's the story they decide to go with. Go figure! When I saw it on the TV, I laughed my ass off."

"You laughed?" Kari asked her. "What was funny about a monumental lie like that?" she asked her.

"The idea of Alex liking kids? He didn't even like his own kids! He hated them, in fact. That why it was so funny."

Alex knew that was the impression people had of him back in the day. That he despised his own daughter and son. But it wasn't true. He loved them dearly, even though they grew up to be spoiled, rich brats who hated him.

But they were getting nowhere with Bridgette. It was obvious that she was a convenient pawn too. But what wasn't so obvious was why bother? Why would they use her name at all? Why was that necessary?

"Anything I can do for you before I leave?" Alex asked her. Once upon a time, they were good friends. Friends with benefits even. But that was a long, long time ago.

Bridgette looked at Alex. She remembered it too. "I need shelter for tonight, man," she said. "Gonna be a storm coming, they say. I don't like sleeping in the rain."

Alex's heart dropped. What a fall from grace she had had! But he was certain it was exactly what she deserved.

Kari thought so too. "What happened to the money?" she asked her.

"That five hundred dollars? Please." She smashed her cigarette in the ashtray. "I'm an addict and an alcoholic, honey. What do you think happened to it? That money was gone as fast as it hit my hand." She looked at Alex. "Are you gonna give me shelter, or not? Or will I have to suck your dick to get something from you? Because all you ever wanted from us ladies anyway was sex. You'd give us diamonds and

142

furs just as long as we slept with you. And when you got bored with us? You showed us the door and never looked back. Forget how it devastated us. Forget that we all fell in love with your rich ass."

Alex already had guilt riding him about his past as it was. Now another casualty he had to deal with. He almost told her to kiss his ass too. But he couldn't do that to her. He stood up and began helping Kari up. "Come on," he said to Bridgette, "let's find you a place to stay."

Bridgette looked up at Alex. "For real?" she asked him.

"Yes. Any place you have in mind?"

Bridgette began rising to her feet. "There's a place not far from here where you can pay by the week for a motel room. If I can get a room for a week, that'll ease a lot of my burdens, man. That's where I want to go."

Alex looked at Kari. She didn't care for Bridgette one bit, but she nodded anyway. Everybody deserved at least a roof over their heads.

"Let's do it," Alex said to Bridgette.

Kari wasn't necessarily onboard with this decision of Alex's, but Kari already figured that Alex knew that woman when she perhaps wasn't so mean and bitter. She held her tongue. And Bridgette got up on unsteady feet, finish the last of her beer, and then began heading, with Alex and Kari, for the exit.

Kari was thinking about what all Bridgette had said as they made their way to the exit. Alex was thinking about it too. And it still wasn't adding up. They still had more questions than answers!

"Excuse me," the waiter said as he squeezed past them in the aisle. And as he squeezed past Bridgette, he reached into his pocket, pulled out a knife, and stabbed her violently threw the heart before even Bridgette realized what had happened to her. Then he began running away.

Alex saw Bridgette's knees give way and

her body began to slump down. But it wasn't until she began falling to the floor did anybody realize she'd been stabbed. One of the waitresses in the bar let out a scream when she saw the blood, and Kari held onto Bridgette's arms, trying to prevent her from hitting her head. Alex anxiously looked over and saw the waiter running away. He immediately realized that waiter was the perpetrator.

"Stay with her!" he yelled to Kari as he began running after that waiter.

"What's happening to me?" Bridgette was crying with nothing but fear in her voice. "What's happening to me?"

It was only then did Kari's heart go out to Bridgette and she cupped her head and laid it on her lap. "It's okay," she said as the blood continued to pour out of her. "You're going to be just fine. Just hold on, okay?"

"Okay," Bridgette said like a child and Kari's heart ached for her. She even took off her blazer and attempted to staunch the blood that wouldn't stop flowing from her knife wound, but even she knew it was like putting a band-aid over an ocean. It was just too much blood!

But Alex was determined to run down that perp, not only because of what he'd done to Bridgette, but because of the answers he might hold to what was actually going on. And why they chose Bridgette. But the perp was younger and far more agile and he was easily getting away.

But Alex had determination on his side and he jumped over tables and threw aside chairs as he matched the young man's gait almost stride for stride. They both were running through the large bar until they were in the back of the bar.

The young man flung open the back door and began running down the steps. But as Alex, too, ran out of that back door, it seemed to him that the perp had slowed considerably, as if he wanted Alex to catch up to him. Or he wanted Alex to know that he could catch up, because he wanted Alex to follow him.

But that was when Alex stopped running on pure adrenalin, and began to think. Was he leading him to a trap?

And then, just after Alex had run down those steps and watched the young man take off across the street, Alex thought again, realizing a different possibility. Maybe the young man wasn't trying to get him to run *to* a trap, but away from one. A trap, not for Alex, but for Kari. For Kari!

Alex's heart fell through his shoes as he turned around so fast he nearly fell, and he began running back up those steps and back into that bar.

Back inside the bar, Kari was still cradling Bridgette when a gunman entered the front of the bar and hurried toward where she and Bridgette were docked. She saw him when he entered, looking casual, but there was something about him that wasn't casual at all. But haunting. And anxious. And when he pulled a magnum from out of his back pocket and began to aim it at Kari, she was not the one. Because when she took off her blazer to help Bridgette's blood flow, she had also pulled out her own piece. A Glock. And she aimed it at that gunman just as he was aiming his at her, but she'd been taught by the best and was a faster gun. She fired first, hitting him before he could fire any round at all. And he slumped to the ground, dropping his gun as the life left his body.

When Alex heard that single gunshot, he nearly died where she stood. And he leaped over a table to get around that corner that would give him eyeshot of Kari.

When he saw that she was okay, he nearly stopped so that his heart could catch back up with his breathing. But suddenly he saw another man, further over in the bar, who was lifting his gun to fire at Kari too. And Kari, Alex could tell, did not see him!

But Alex saw him and he didn't delay. He

had his magnum already locked and loaded and in his hands, too, and he ran toward the man firing his weapon repeatedly. His aim was precise, as he wasn't going to hit any innocent bystander, but he wanted to make sure he took that motherfucker out.

And he did. Repeatedly. The gunman was already dead by the time Alex fired his second shot.

Kari was stunned. She hadn't seen the second gunman at all! And she and Alex both began to look around. Was that place still hot? Were there other gunmen in the shadows of that shadowy bar?

But once Alex was satisfied that all was clear, he hurried over to Kari and Bridgette. Bridgette's eyes were wide open, but was she still with them? Alex looked at Kari. Kari shook her head.

And they both just stayed there, stunned, as sirens could be heard in the background.

What in the world just happened, they

both wanted to know?

But they couldn't even begin to process any of it because the police arrived shortly after Alex had shot the second gunman, and they questioned Alex and Kari, separately, for nearly five hours. When several innocent bar customers came forward and told exactly what had happened, they were free to go. No charges would be filed.

But when they got into their SUV, and their driver drove them to Alex's plane, they couldn't help but think about what took place.

Kari was so intensely trying to make reason out of what had happened that she didn't realize Alex was holding her hand until he was squeezing it. And she looked at him. "What was that about, Alex?" she asked him. "Was that press conference a set up to get you here?"

"That's how I'm seeing it too," said Alex.

"But they were going after me, not after you," Kari said. "How would they know that you'd take me with you?"

"I don't think they knew initially," Alex said. "They might have developed that part of their plan after they saw you board my plane with me. I think the main plan was for me to chase the waiter that stabbed Bridgette into that alley. But you were on the scene too. I think they decided to set traps for both of us."

Kari frowned. This was getting to be too much for her to bear. "But why?" she asked him.

"Because somebody wants me to suffer. Taking you out would have done the trick. That's why they tried it at that Fair. Apparently, they didn't have a high degree of confidence that they could take me out that easily."

"Which means they have to know you on that level," Kari said.

Kari, Alex realized, was on to something. "Which means," he said, "they would have known me during my days in my father's crime syndicate. Before I came to America. When it was my job to do all that kind of twisted shit."

Kari nodded. "But does that narrow it

down for you?" she asked him.

Alex leaned his head back in frustration, and he closed his eyes. "Narrow it? Hell no," he said. "That expands it."

Kari let out a frustrated exhale herself. And she leaned her head back too. Then she cuddled against Alex, and he wrapped his arms around her. But he still was nowhere near the why of it all. Nowhere near it.

CHAPTER SIXTEEN

Back at the penthouse and in bed, Kari was on top of Alex and Alex was deep inside of her, but it was more of a work-it-out than a lovemaking session for both of them. Alex was pumping so hard and holding Kari so tight as he fucked her that she thought she wouldn't be able to endure it. Both of them were moaning and feeling the intensity as their sweat-filled bodies began to reach the zenith. And when they came, it was more of a stress release than an exhilaration. They had too much on their minds.

Alex remained inside of Kari and Kari remained on top of Alex after they came, and both of them continued to just lay there. They both had already taken peeps at the baby monitor. Angela, with her two nannies in the nursery with her, was still sound asleep. But Alex, Kari noticed as she continued to hold him, was shivering.

She leaned up and looked at him. "Are you okay?"

It was obvious he wasn't okay. His entire body seemed strained. "What are they after, Karena?" he asked with deep frustration in his voice.

"What about the woman in Provence? What did she say?"

"She said she didn't know what it was either. She just knew it would be harmful to me."

"Maybe it had something to do with Bridgette," said Kari. "Why else would they have used her?"

Alex shook his head. "There was nothing to that relationship. Nothing worth remembering anyway."

"But what about that time in your life when you were seeing Bridgette? Was something going on then?"

Alex shook his head again. "No. Nothing. At least nothing I can recall."

"We have to think more strategically,

Alex. Is there something in your past that you may not think was a big deal, but that stands out as something more than the normal?"

"Goodness yes," said Alex. "Millions of somethings."

Kari hated to hear that. "But something really bad," she said. "Something horrific. That can't be in the millions."

"The thousands then," said Alex. Then he laid her head back down on his chest. "Stop trying to figure it out, Karena. My past is like a rabbit hole. There's deep shit everywhere. I wouldn't know where to begin."

Kari closed her eyes. She married no saint. She knew that going in. And boy was that true now.

CHAPTER SEVENTEEN

The next morning at breakfast, Kari was at the kitchen table with the baby on her lap feeding her, while Gloria was seated at the table rubbing her ever-expanding belly.

"When did you get back in town?" Kari asked her.

"Late last night. Oz flew in on his plane and came and got me. He showed up at Dad's door eleven at night talking about let's go home."

"And you came home."

Gloria nodded. "And I came home."

"Is that why you run home to Daddy? So Oz can come and get you?"

"That's not the reason, no. I just get tired of the neglect and the lack of seriousness. He parties too much for a man his age. And when I remind his ass that we have a child on the way and he's got to settle himself down before the child gets here, he can't be bothered by all of that. He's nothing like Mr. Drakos!"

Kari looked at Gloria. "Of course he's not. And you knew that from jump."

Gloria acknowledged it with a nod of her head. "Yes, I knew it. I knew I was marrying a man whose personality couldn't be contained. I knew that. And I have given Oz so much leeway, Kari. I don't try to box him in. But he's beginning to take advantage of that leeway. He's . . ." Gloria didn't continue.

Kari wiped Angela's mouth as she looked at Gloria. "He's what?" When Gloria didn't continue, Kari guessed. "Is another woman involved, Glo?" she asked her pointblank.

Gloria hunched her small shoulders. "He says there isn't another woman."

"But you don't believe him?"

"I just don't know! He's gone so much."

"Then your ass needs to start going with him," Kari said. "Belly and all. Because one thing's for sure: you can't keep running home to Daddy when that baby gets here. You can't do that to your child. You'd better find out exactly what Oz is up to, if he's up to anything, and you'd better make up your mind if you can live with that. Because depending on a man like Oz changing is a fool's errand. He's not going to change."

Gloria exhaled. "Deep down I know that's true. But I still believe he can settle down at least."

"Settle down to what? A nine-to-five? A homebody?" Kari shook her head. "Oz has the kind of outsized personality that will never belong to one person or one lifestyle. He'll always belong to the world. That's just the way he is. People gravitate to him. All kinds of people."

"Including women is what you're saying," said Gloria.

"All kinds of people," Kari said as she looked over and saw that Alex had come downstairs, fully dressed in his business suit when she was still in her bathrobe, and he was coming into the kitchen. "Good morning," she said.

Alex grunted. He was not a morning person.

Gloria smiled when she saw him. "Good morning, Mr. Drakos." He was a man she greatly admired and loved.

"You're back," Alex said to her.

"Yes, sir."

"Stay this time."

Gloria realized he had just said to her in three words what Kari was saying to her during their entire conversation. "I'll try, sir."

But Alex's gruff exterior turned far more pleasant when he knelt down to kiss Angela. Angela flapped her hands and grinned at her father. "How's my little angel?" he asked her.

"Say I'm hungry, that's what I am," Kari said.

Alex kissed his daughter again and then

looked up at Kari. They both could see the emotional exhaustion on each other's face. Alex kissed her on the lips and, as he began standing, whispered in her ear: "It'll be okay."

They exchanged another glance as Jordan came into the kitchen in a pair of shorts and socks. "Ma, what happened to my blue hoodie? Ma?"

"Good morning," Alex said to his son.

"Oh, hey Dad. Hey, Glo. I mean, Aunt Gloria. Ma, what happened to my blue hoodie?"

"I threw that thing away."

Jordan was stunned. "*Why*?"

"Because it has twenty thousand holes in it, Jordan."

"But I was gonna wear it after school today. Matty's having a basketball game at his house."

"No school for you today," said Alex.

Jordan looked at him. "No school?"

"No. You stay here under strict security. Nobody goes anywhere without my authorization."

"But Dad, I have an exam today."

"Get it rescheduled."

"But why can't I just go and take it and then come back home?"

Kari could see Alex's patience wearing thin. "Because I said so, Jordan," Alex said.

But Jordan didn't see it. "But why?" he asked again.

"Because I said so!" Alex exploded. "That's why!"

Jordan and Gloria both jumped at Alex's harshly raised voice, and even the smile on Angela's face quickly faded as her innocent brown face stared at her father. Kari and Alex both could see the hurt in their sensitive son's eyes when Alex exploded on him, but before anybody could say anything Jordan hurried out of the kitchen.

Alex hated to have lost his cool that way, and he knew it wasn't Jordan's fault at all. But it was the kind of mood he was in. "I'll be in my office," Alex said as he began heading out of the kitchen. He looked back at Kari. "You and Angie stay indoors today, too, unless you get permission from me. You hear me?"

Kari continued to feed Angela.

Alex stopped and looked at her. "You hear me, Karena?"

"Yes!" Her nerves were on edge too. She looked at him. "I heard you."

Alex felt a sudden pang of guilt for putting his family through all of the trials and tribulations he was always putting them through. They deserved better than him, and he knew it. He left the kitchen.

But as he headed for the front door of their penthouse, he thought about Jordan and the sadness in his eyes. He had adopted the best kid in the world, a young man Kari, as a fifteen-year-old single mother, had raised right. He deserved better too. And instead of leaving, Alex went to Jordan's room.

Jordan was on the edge of his bed

playing a video game. It was the way guys his age alleviated stress, Alex assumed, although he found playing those things nothing but stress-provoking rather than alleviating. He sat down on the bed beside Jordan.

"I was out of line, son," Alex said to him. "I apologize for taking my frustration out of you."

"No need to apologize to me," Jordan said, although Alex could see he was still pissed with him.

"There is a need," Alex said.

"Whatever," Jordan said.

Alex could see that Jordan's eyes were bright with unshed tears. That press conference with that so-called Bridgette Venew had shaken him, probably to his core, and they needed to deal with that.

Alex placed his arm around Jordan. "Everything at that press conference was a pack of lies," he said to him. "That woman wasn't Bridgette Venew, and I didn't even know the real Bridgette when she was twelve years old. It was all lies, Jordan."

"I know that," Jordan said as he continued to attack his game. "But you have a lot of women after you." He said this and then glanced over at Alex.

Alex wasn't going to deny it. "Yes," he said.

"They used to call you the Billionaire Playboy," Jordan reminded him.

Alex wasn't going to deny that either. "That's true," he said.

Then a tear escaped Jordan's eyes beneath his glasses. He pushed them up on his nose. "Are you gonna leave us?" he asked him.

Alex frowned, and pulled Jordan closer against him. "No! Never. Why would you think that, J?"

Then Alex wrapped both arms around him, and Jordan stopped playing his game. "You and your mother and Angie are my life. I'll never leave any of you. Never."

"Not even for a woman prettier than

Mom?"

Alex smiled. "There is no woman prettier than Mom."

Jordan smiled and wiped his tears away. "If Ma was here, she'd say bullshit."

Alex smiled, and then laughed. "Yes, she would, wouldn't she?" he said.

But then he thought about how little they still knew about what was going on, and his joy was greatly tempered.

He kissed Jordan on the top of his head. "You're a good son, Jordan," he said.

Jordan smiled. "Thanks, Dad," he responded. And then they heard the commotion.

"Alex! Kari! Alex!"

It was Oz. He had just run into the house. Alex and Jordan ran into the foyer, while Gloria and Kari, carrying Angela, ran out into the living room. They all converged together to see just what had Oz so hysterical.

"What is it?" Kari anxiously asked him.

Oz took a moment to compose himself. And then he exhaled. "We just lost The Drakos Corporation," he said. Then he looked at Alex. "We've literally just lost billions."

Everybody was staring at Oz. But when they heard that incredible, earth-shattering news, all eyes flew to Alex. But it was so stunning to Alex, too, and such a shock to everything he knew to be right in this world, that he became motionless. And then it hit him. It hit him like a sledgehammer. Because that news made him realize, right then and there, what was really going on.

CHAPTER EIGHTEEN

With Oz refusing to leave the hotel and casino, which were separate entities from Alex's company, he and Gloria stayed back with the baby. Oz was convinced whoever took over The Drakos Corporation could try something on that end, and he was keeping all hands on deck. But while he remained at the home front, Alex, Kari, and Jordan boarded Alex's plane for New York and left Florida in a daze. Jordan needed to be there since he would one day run the company if they ever got it back, and he needed to know what to do should something like this ever happened under his watch. But Alex was keeping his own counsel. He wasn't in any condition to school anybody on anything at that moment.

Kari and Jordan understood his unrelenting shock. A man who worked his lifetime to build up a corporation, only to have it legally stolen from him overnight didn't need advice from them. They remained silent, too. But Kari was praying that it was all some kind of cruel hoax.

When the plane landed at LaGuardia, they hurried down the airstairs and eventually jumped into a waiting SUV. Three other SUVs were also present, as security, and they followed the lead vehicle through the streets of Manhattan to The Drakos Corporation. To avoid the press, who was already out in force about the Bridgette Venew affair, and now this, they headed around back to a private, gated entrance.

It may have seemed as if Alex was in a

fog, and he was, but he still had the presence of mind to take Kari's hand and hold it tight and to put an arm around Jordan's waist as they made their way through the revolving doors of the mammoth office building. The usually bustling place felt like a funeral inside. Everybody were still in shock. And by the time they took the private elevator to the top floor, and made it into Alex's suite of offices, all of his senior executives and staff were piled into his office still reeling from the news too. And still watching the various television screens where CNBC, Bloomberg, FOX Business and three more around-the-clock news outlets were all talking about the incredible fall and takeover of Alex Drakos's company. They all were also mentioning that Bridgette Venew fiasco as well.

"How could this happen," asked the head of logistics. "That's what I wanna know! How could this have possibly happened?"

"We let the Sterling Group steal it right from under us," said the COO. "I've already scheduled a board meeting. We've got to get to the bottom of this!"

"And who is this Sterling Group anyway?" asked the head of accounting. "I've never heard of such a group."

"Alex," asked his long time CFO Matthew Scribner, who used to be Matt Stafford before he married a woman who asked him to take on her last name, "how could this be? How in hell could you not see this coming?"

But Kari took offense to that question. "Why didn't you see it coming, Matthew?" she asked him. "How dare you blame Alex for this shit. You're the chief financial officer for this corporation. Where the hell were you?"

Everybody looked at Matt as if Kari was saying out loud what they were all thinking too. But Alex wasn't looking to blame anybody. The buck always stopped with him. He was pacing the floor, his hands in his pockets, his head down in deep contemplation even as his CFO attempted to defend himself, and even as more questions and recriminations were tossed back and forth as if nobody was going to take the blame for this one. Until Kari, who was studying her husband the entire time, asked the only pertinent question. "What is this really about, Alex?" she asked him.

Alex finally stopped in his tracks. He didn't look at his wife. He didn't look at anybody, as if he was still trying to figure it all out in his own head. He was staring straight ahead. "That bright, shiny object," he said. "That's what it's about."

They all looked at him. Kari knew what he meant, but she needed clarity on why he was saying it. "Your past?" she asked him.

Alex looked at her. He never had to go around the world explaining to Kari. She got him. And he nodded his head. "That whole story about having dirt on me from my past and having that press conference with that fake Bridgette Venew and those women warning me about danger ahead because of my past was a bright shiny object to keep my attention away from what was going on with my company."

"But that's why you pay these motherfuckers," Kari said, looking around at all of those highly paid white men gathered in that office. "There were no shiny objects in their faces. Where were they? Why weren't they paying attention?"

Alex looked at them too. But mainly he looked at Matt Scribner, his CFO. But Matt still refused to bear any of the blame. "We did everything we could," he said. "They weren't showing their hand weeks or even days ahead of time. They showed nothing. We were taking little hits for a few weeks, yes we were, but I was telling you about those hits."

"You were also telling him it was nothing to worry about," said Kari.

"Because it wasn't!"

"That's a *got*damn lie," Kari said. "Those little hits turned into an entire takeover! How the fuck was that nothing to worry about?!"

Jordan and the other men in the room nodded their heads. Other than Alex, Kari was the only one who was ever willing to go toe-to-toe with that arrogant CFO bastard. And they all were more than happy that she was doing it. Because he should have seen this coming had he been on the job. But what they didn't understand was why Alex hadn't lit into his ass yet too. But Alex seemed as if his mind was a million miles away.

And it was. Because he still couldn't figure it out. He needed to put the pieces together and find out who was really behind the takeover to begin with. "Who runs the Sterling Group?" he asked.

"You mean who are they?" asked Matt.

"Who sits at the top?" Alex asked.

"We're still trying to find that out, sir," said the COO. "We just don't know at this point."

But then his cell phone rang. He didn't realize Kari had it (he had dropped it on the plane and didn't notice) until she pulled it out of her purse and looked at the Caller ID. She answered it quickly. "Angie okay?" she asked.

It was Oz. "She's fine. Put my brother on the phone."

Kari handed the phone to Alex. "Oz," she said.

"Angie okay?" Alex asked as he was taking the phone.

"She's okay," Kari said.

"The hotel and casino alright?" Alex asked as soon as he answered the call.

"Everything's fine on this end," said Oz. "It's that fucking Sterling Group."

This interested Alex. "What do you know?"

"I know who's behind it."

"Who?" Alex asked.

"Guy name Dimitri Kalashnik. A member of the Russian mob, although I don't know him. Never heard of him."

But when Alex heard that name he went still. Everybody in the room saw the abrupt

174

change in him.

"What is it, Dad?" Jordan asked him.

"Alex, what is it?" asked Matt.

"You know him?" Oz asked over the phone.

Alex knew him alright. "He's with the Russian outfit," Alex said, "but he has Greek roots. Look in both areas. But find him," Alex said. "Find that motherfucker."

"I've got men on the case already," said Oz. "I'll find his ass. But who is he to you, Alex?"

"I'll tell you about it later," he said to his brother, and ended the call.

But he couldn't that easily dismiss the room. Especially a room with Kari in it. "Oz found out who's behind the Sterling Group?" she asked him.

Alex nodded. "Yes."

"Who?" asked Matt.

"Dimitri Kalashnik."

"Who's that?" his COO asked. "I've never heard that name before."

Alex exhaled. "He's a member of the Russian Oligarch. One of the bosses."

Everybody got nervous and began looking at each other. The oligarchs were considered in business circles to be a code name for mob. They all heard rumors about Alex's past mob connections back in his home country of Greece. They never wanted any association with any of that.

But Kari was still staring at Alex. There was more to the story than he was telling. "Jordan, clear the room," she said to their son.

And Jordan began doing just that. The men were pissed that some kid was telling them what to do, but they also knew that that kid could be their boss one day. Besides, they wanted plausible deniability if anything negative came out about that Sterling Group and Alex. They left without incident.

But Alex stopped Matt. "Matthew?" he said to his CFO.

Matt turned around. "Yes?"

"You're fired," Alex said.

Matt was stunned. He stared at Alex. It had to be a board decision, but he knew the board would go along with whatever Alex wanted. If they even still had a board!

But Jordan was easing him on out. "You heard my father," Jordan said.

Matt walked on out, looking as if he was in a daze, and Jordan closed the door behind him. And then went back over to his parents.

"Alex, who is he?" Kari was asking.

"He's a member of the Russian mob."

"You told us that already," Kari said. "Don't give me that official shit. Who is he? Because you know him. Don't you?"

Alex finally looked at Kari. "Yes," he admitted.

"Who is he?" Kari asked again. Then she got to the point. "What did you do to him?" she asked.

Alex hesitated again. But he answered her question. "I killed his wife," he said.

CHAPTER NINETEEN

"I thought I was in love with her," Alex said to Kari and Jordan as they stood stunned in his office. He stole the man's wife, and then killed her too? Did they hear him right? There had to be some mistake!

But if there was, Alex wasn't telling it. He, instead, was telling them the facts. No spin. "I wasn't in love with her, now that I know what love is. But I thought so at the time."

He paused. But then he continued. "Her

name was Nadia Smirnoff," he said. "Beautiful girl. But I was married to my first wife. And Nadia was married as well."

"She was married to Dimitri Kalashnik?" Kari asked, putting the pieces together.

Alex nodded. "Yes."

But Jordan had a different question. "Did you have an affair with her while you were still married to your first wife?" he asked. "Or was it after the divorce?" It would give him the first insight into whether Alex was also capable of cheating on his mother.

Alex didn't deny it. "Yes," he said. "We had an affair during my marriage. And hers."

Kari's heart dropped a little, but she couldn't stay in that emotion. She needed to know what was going on. "You were in love with her you said?"

"Yes. Or at least I thought so at the time."

"How did you meet her?"

Alex hesitated. "We worked on an acquisition together overseas."

It sounded so familiar to Jordan and Kari. "So you started cheating on your wife on a business trip?" Jordan asked.

Alex was beyond denials. "Yes," he said.

Jordan looked at his mother. All of her fears were being realized! But Kari kept her eye on the ball. "What happened?" she asked Alex. Jordan was stunned that she wasn't cussing him out.

Alex was keeping his eye on the ball too. Because that ball contained dynamite. And Kari and Jordan had to know the full story in order for him to contain it. "I found out she had cheated me."

"You mean she cheated on you?" Jordan asked. "With who? Her husband?"

"No, she didn't cheat on me," said Alex. "She cheated me. Out of nearly forty million dollars. Thirty-nine million and eight-hundred-thousand to be precise."

Kari and Jordan both were stunned. *Thirty-nine million dollars?* They were floored.

"How?" Kari asked him.

"By overvaluing, by nearly fifty million bucks, the company we acquired shares in. I paid the extra as majority owner, while she got thirty-nine million of the fifty-million extra. The company she was in cahoots with got the remaining millions. She was a snake in Versace."

"What happened to her?" Kari asked, getting concerned.

"I did what we did back then. She betrayed me. I did what we did to rats."

Jordan was shocked. "You killed the woman you loved just because she cheated you out of some money?" he asked.

Kari wanted to correct her son. Thirty-nine million dollars wasn't *some money*. It was a fortune! But she knew that would send the wrong message. Because Jordan was right. Was money worth losing your life over?

But a pained look came over Alex's face. "It wasn't about the money," Alex said. "It was about the betrayal. I couldn't let that stand or other fools would try me on every hand. I bombed her car," he said. "It was supposed to be an easy in and out."

Kari's heart began to tighten. "But it wasn't?"

"It was," said Alex. But his look said differently.

"But what happened?" Kari asked.

Alex didn't want to even verbalize it. But he knew he had. "I didn't know her little girls were in the car with her," he said.

Jordan covered his mouth in total shock. Kari was knocked for a loop too. They both could not believe what they were hearing.

"You said girls," Kari said. "There was more than one?"

"There were two at the time," Alex said. "The bomb, no, *I* killed them both by planting that bomb underneath that car."

Kari was shaken by that revelation. Two little girls? She had to sit down. Jordan helped her to a seat. And he held onto that seat too. He couldn't stop staring at his father. Was this man capable of something that heinous?

"Surely it wasn't you, Dad. You hired somebody, right? You ordered that hit, right?"

But Alex was shaking his head and looking Jordan dead in the eyes. "No, son," he said with anguish in his own eyes. "I handled that assignment personally."

Jordan's heart dropped. And that look in his eyes, and in Kari's eyes, did him in.

"How could you not remember something like that, Alex?" Kari asked him. "I kept asking you to think about something horrific in your past. Two children were killed, and that didn't come to your mind?"

"No," said Alex.

"But why not?" asked Kari.

"Because I still had my foot in the mob. Because I still had that shit so deep inside of me I didn't know how to handle situations any other way. Because there were dozens, even hundreds of other situations where I had to take out whole families who tried to take out mine, or me, or my businesses. That shit wasn't unusual. It was routine! That's the kind of world I once occupied. That's the world I once ruled. Now it's coming back for me."

Jordan had to sit down too. It was too much to take. He knew his father had been in the mob before. He knew he had all kinds of mob connections still. But Alex was a moral man. The most moral, ethical man he knew. How could he have ever been that person? And was he still that person?

That was the question for Jordan. For Kari, too, if she were to be honest. And they both found themselves at a loss for words. They found themselves staring at the man they loved. And judging Alex.

And Alex felt their judgment to the roots of his core. And he couldn't take it. Not from them. Not from the people he most loved in the world. His baby girl was too young to know. But one day she'd be judging him too.

He left. He walked out of his own office and left. But when he saw the security detail that stood outside his door, and they began to follow him, he stopped and looked at them. "Stay with my family," he ordered. And they all stayed where they were as Alex left alone.

Back in the office, Jordan was looking at his mother with nothing but pain in his eyes. Because she looked devastated. How were they ever going to come back from this, he wondered?

But Kari had already signed up for this. She knew who she was marrying. She knew he had a past that stunk-up the place. Her eyes were wide open.

And she hurried out of that office. She ran for her man.

Jordan didn't know what she was doing. But he followed her anyway. And Security followed them.

When they made it downstairs and

around to the private entrance, Alex's SUV was just pulling off.

Kari, along with Jordan, jumped into the second SUV. "Follow my husband!" she ordered as her Security detail jumped in the SUV too.

And the driver, already told that an order from Kari Grant-Drakos was the same as an order from Alex Drakos himself, did as he was told. He followed the SUV that was carrying Alex.

They got caught up in that heavy New York traffic and couldn't keep up with Alex's SUV early on, but it was obvious to Kari, by the direction his SUV had been going, where Alex was heading.

Besides, she knew her husband. She knew him better than anybody alive.

"Go to Hudson Valley," she ordered, when they were stalled in traffic and Alex's SUV was long gone.

CHAPTER TWENTY

He hurried to the full-sized bar inside his home and poured himself a tall glass of whiskey. And he frowned just thinking about it again. The look of disgust on their faces would haunt him for the rest of his life. Even tough-as-nails Kari was disgusted with him. And poor Jordan. He looked as if he'd lost his hero forever. He looked as if everything he thought Alex was turned out to be lies. And Alex could hardly deal with that. He took another long drink.

What he did, at the time, was what they did to traitors and thieves. And if innocents were lost in the process, it was always the traitor's fault. Her ass wouldn't have stolen from him, then her children would not have been caught in the game. That was how he was raised. That was always the rule. It was those kind of rules that caused Alex to walk away from the game a long, long time ago.

Because what he did, in the light of day, was so deplorable to him now that it was sickening to him. He wasn't that person anymore. And after saying out loud what he had done, and saying it to his own family, a part of him was having a hard time believing that he was ever that person.

But as he thought about it, and took another swallow of whiskey, he heard the door to his home open. Which shocked him. He sat his glass down and grabbed the loaded magnum he kept under the bar counter. He was about to head toward the entrance to confront the intruder, until he heard Kari's voice.

"Alex?" she yelled. "Alex?"

Alex was stunned. Was that Karena? Kari was here? Had something happened already?

He immediately put the gun back under the counter and made his way toward the entrance, his heart pounding in anticipation. Was she alright? What about Jordan? Angie? Did something happen after he left?

And then he saw her and Jordan as they entered the living room area where he was. And that look of disgust was no longer on their faces. A look of deep concern, concern for him, was all he saw.

"Alex!" Kari said as she and Jordan ran to him.

When they slammed their small bodies against his big, muscular frame, and when they wrapped their arms around him as if he were still their hero, a part of Alex melted in love. He could hardly believe how fortunate he was to have a family like them. And he wrapped his arms around them too.

They all held back tears as they held onto each other. And then Kari looked up at him. "Thought you got rid of us, didn't you?" she asked.

Alex smiled. Leave it to Kari to come to his rescue. "I tried," he said. "But I'm like gum under a shoe. I'll always find a way to stick around."

Kari smiled. And then laughed. Jordan looked up at his father. "That is so not funny, Dad," he said. "Kind of gross actually."

"Really?" Alex was still smiling.

"For real, though." Jordan was happy, but he couldn't bring himself to smile at that ridiculous joke.

But when their eyes met, their hearts went out to each other as if that bond was not broken nor could it ever be broken. And Jordan laid his head back on his father's chest and held him tighter.

Alex pulled him closer. And he pulled Kari closer too.

Yep, he thought, as he held onto his family. Just like gum under a shoe.

NOTHING LEFT TO LOSE

CHAPTER TWENTY-ONE

They stayed the night in New York at their Hudson Valley estate, and Alex spent most of that night deep inside of Kari. They were both naked in bed, both turned on their sides with Kari's back to Alex's front, and his penis was still fully aroused and still moving slowly inside of her. It wasn't about cumming for either one of them. It wasn't even about relaxing their raw nerves. It was all about feeling the love they had for each other, and the connection they had to each other.

For Kari, it was a sense that their world had been impacted, and it threw them for a big-ass loop, but it didn't break them.

But it was more than that for her too. She saw the meddle of the man she married. She saw Alex at one of his lowest points, where he lost the lion's share of his fortune, a fortune that was tied up in his corporate entities, but he was more devastated by how she and Jordan responded to what happened in his past than to that monumental loss. It showed Kari what mattered most to Alex. It wasn't the money. It wasn't the prestige and power. It was them. His family.

For Alex, it was all about redemption. He loved how they heard what kind of man he used to be but still came to him. He loved that he had a true ride or die family. But he still couldn't get over the looks on their faces when they first heard what he'd done. How he brought that retribution on himself. He had to set that right and take Dimitri's ass out. He knew he had to do that. But he also knew he had to redeem himself in the eyes of his family. He had to do better by them. He had to make them see that he was nothing like the man he used to be, even though he knew he had to become that man again to get his company back. And he was getting his company back. He exhaled. It was a daunting task. He had work to do on every front.

But Kari heard that frustrated exhale. And she reached back and touched Alex. "You're okay?" she asked him.

"A lot to do," Alex admitted.

"What's the game plan?"

"Redeem myself in the eyes of my family. And I already know what you're going to say."

"Oh, yeah? And what's that?"

"You don't think I need redeeming."

"Like hell I don't." Kari was still her blunt self. "You need it. Not in my eyes so much, but definitely in Jordan's eyes. He loves you, but that news shook him, Alex. It shook him to his core. He didn't think you were capable of something that terrible."

"What about you?" Alex asked. "Aren't you just as shaken?"

Kari shook her head. "I've seen you in action, remember? I know what your ass is capable of. I knew it before I married you. But I married you anyway. What does that say about me?"

"That you're just as hardcore as I am," Alex said, and they both laughed.

But then he wrapped his arms around her and kissed her on the side of her face. And his penis began to become more active inside of her. His movements began to increase.

"Where do we go from here?" Kari asked.

"Oz has our guys searching for Dimitri's ass. When he finds him, I'll deal with him."

"Get your company back first, Alex," Kari said. "And then get your revenge. In that order. Keep emotion out of it."

"Your ass trying to tell me what to do?" Alex asked as he began to feel the emotion of his penis inside of her.

"I'm not *trying* to tell you," said Kari. "I'm telling you what to do."

"In that case," said Alex, his gyrations increasing even more, "I'll have to take it out on somebody. Since I'm slapping the shit out of your ass right now, it may as well be you."

Kari laughed as Alex pulled her tighter against him and began to pound into her with such force and precision that her laughter ended, and her passion began. Because she was feeling it too. And the harder he did her, the harder she felt it. Until they were both riding the tiger. Until they were both so caught up in the throes of their passion that they were moaning and groaning and Kari was holding onto Alex's hair from behind and Alex was pulling Kari closer to against his chest as he felt the oncoming surge. And then it broke free. For both of them. And they came. Both of them.

Kari arched and Alex strained and they released that tension, that worry, that monumental work they had in front of them, and left it all between the sheets.

And when their sweaty bodies finally came to rest, and Alex finally pulled out of Kari, immediately making her feel as if she was losing him again, she turned to him. She had to see his face. And what she suspected she'd see was true. The anguish was still in his eyes.

He was lying on his back. She leaned over and turned his face to her. "You did what you had to do back then, Alex," she said to him. "That chick stole, not only your heart, but nearly forty million dollars from you. What did her ass expect was going to happen?"

"And those children?" Alex said to Kari so softly that Kari felt his heartbreak.

"You didn't know what you didn't know," Kari said. "It's awful. It is awful. But it happened. What can you do about it now? Let Dimitri Kalashnik keep your company because of what you did to his wife and children? Decide that you guys are even now? Or do you fight like hell and get your company back? And handle him for taking it in the first place because if you don't handle him, it'll give our other enemies ideas."

Alex frowned. "It's a vicious cycle, Karena."

Kari nodded, and frowned too. "Yes, it is,"

she said regrettably. "But what you gonna do, Alex? It is what it is." Then she added: "And you are who you are."

Alex looked at her, as if he needed confirmation.

She gave it to him. "And you are not some monster," she said. "You're a good man caught in bad situations. And you either fight or give up. We both know what you're going to do."

Alex inwardly smiled. If everybody on the face of this earth gave up on him, he knew Kari wouldn't. He knew Kari Drakos would have his back.

He pulled her into his arms.

And even as he thought about what lie ahead for them, he still knew he could bear it, and go through it, with Kari by his side.

CHAPTER TWENTY-TWO

The next day, Kari was in her office meeting with the housekeeping supervisors. They were all standing in front of her desk, and she was standing behind her desk. And she was livid.

"Trip Advisor has a horrible review. Have you seen it?"

"We saw it," said Sharon, the head of Housekeeping.

"Blood on the sheets," Kari said. "Throw up on the toilet rim? Are you kidding me?"

"It was one room," said Sharon, "and only one guest."

Kari couldn't believe she said that. "*What*?" she asked incredulously.

"We dropped the ball on that one room, yes we did. But that doesn't define this hotel."

"How would you feel had that been you on holiday and you were the one who booked that one particular room? How would you have felt, Share?"

"I would have felt bad, but what I'm saying is that it's just one room. That doesn't define who we are."

"Of course it doesn't. And for the vast majority of the people, it won't. But that guest had a horrible experience. That's on us. That's on you and your department."

"It won't happen again. I promise you that."

But Kari was shaking her head. "That's not good enough. No ma'am. I told you every time a room is cleaned it has to be checked. And I mean glove-checked. Had it been checked, your staff would have seen the throw-up on the toilet rim. That throw-up would have given them cause to throw the covers back and expect that bed and everything else. But it wasn't checked at all. How many more rooms weren't checked? No, Sharon, telling me it won't happen again gives me no reassurance. You're fired," Kari said.

All of the supervisors were shocked. And most of those same supervisors were pleased. Sharon had been dropping the ball a lot lately.

But Sharon was angry. "Fired? Over *that*? That was nothing!"

"That's why your ass don't deserve to be here," Kari said. "Your services are no longer needed. You will receive a generous severance package that will tie you over until you're able to find a new job. But you're getting out of here."

"I'm fired? You're *firing* me? After what's been happening with that husband of yours you want to fire *me*?" Then she jumped defiant. "I'll be glad to go. From what I read in the papers, y'all won't be owning The Drakos much longer anyway. I'll be glad to go," she said again, and left the office, slamming the door behind her.

The other supervisors looked worried. But Kari reassured them. "The Drakos is a separate entity from The Drakos Corporation. Your jobs are secure. Paulette, you're acting

Head until I make a decision."

"Yes, ma'am," Paulette said happily, and the rest of the supervisors seemed pleased with that move too.

"Now get back to work," Kari said, and they left.

Kari sat down and leaned her head back. She hated making those kind of life-altering decisions, but she had no problem doing it because the hotel came first. And the one thing she would never compromise on was cleanliness. The Drakos had always gotten very near perfect ratings for cleanliness. She aimed to keep it that way.

But then her door was quickly opened and Bud, the GM, came hurrying just behind Carla, one of Kari's maids.

"It's not true," Bud said before the maid could open her mouth.

"It is true!" the maid said to Kari.

"I told them you were busy," said Kari's secretary, who ran in behind them.

"It's okay," Kari said to her secretary. What now, she thought? "What's this about?" she asked Bud.

"It's about what he did to me, Miss Kari," Carla, instead, answered.

Kari's heart dropped. Not a sexual harassment allegation. Not now at a time like this! "What did he do to you?" she asked the maid.

"He slapped me, and he slapped me right in front of the guests. That's an assault. That's a crime!"

"Stop being so hysterical," Bud said.

Kari looked at him. "You're saying she's lying?"

"That's exactly what I'm saying!"

"Where did this happen?" Kari asked.

"In the hallway just outside his office. He got mad at me because I told off one of those high rollers in the casino for groping me. And he slapped me."

"When did it happen?"

"It just happened," Carla said.

Kari stood up and looked at her secretary. "Contact Security. Tell them I want footage from within the last hour outside the GM's office."

"Yes, ma'am," the secretary said and quickly left the office.

Kari looked at the GM. "Don't waste my time, Bud. What am I going to see? Am I going to see you slap this girl?"

The GM hesitated. And then he came clean. "Yes," he said. "But her ass deserved it."

Kari couldn't believe he said that. "Because she wouldn't let a man *grope* her?"

"Because he was just playing around."

"That wasn't no playing!" Carla complained.

"He was playing around!" said the GM again.

Kari couldn't believe it. She didn't have time for this! "Apologize to her," she said to Bud.

But Bud shook his head. "I'm not

apologizing to shit. For what? I don't see where I did anything wrong."

"You assaulted me!" Carla said. "You put your hands on me. That's illegal!"

Kari could see a lawsuit coming if she didn't handle it right and handle it right now. "Apologize to her," she said, "or your employment with this organization will be terminated."

Although Carla was glad to hear the news, Bud couldn't believe his ears. "What the fuck are you talking about?" he asked her. "You can't fire me!"

Kari hadn't expected that response. "Excuse me?"

"I said you can't fire me. You're nothing but a maid yourself. That's what you were when Alex rescued you. And you're talking about firing *me*? I don't work for your ass."

"Are you out of your mind?"

It was a new voice in the mix, and everybody turned toward the office entrance.

Everybody, especially the GM, was shocked to see Alex standing there in his designer suit, looking so smug it seemed to the GM, with his hands in his pockets.

Alex pushed away from the doorjamb and began walking further into the office. "Do you realize who this lady is?" he asked his GM.

Bud wasn't as formidable anymore now that Alex was on the scene. He hesitated. "Yes, sir, I know who she is."

"She's my wife," Alex said. "She's Mrs. Alex Drakos. And the power that I've invested in her is absolute. She can fire me, that's the kind of power she has." Then Alex frowned. "And if she can fire me, what the fuck you think she can do to you?"

Carla wanted to smile. It was the first time she'd ever seen anybody put Mr. Bud in his place.

But Bud was in shock. "I didn't do anything wrong."

"She said you did. I take her word for it.

Get out. She fired you, you're fired. Get out."

Alex said it in no uncertain terms, and Bud got it then. He gave Kari a hard stare, but he knew, because Alex confirmed it, there was nothing he could do about it. He left the office.

Alex moved away from the desk, rubbing the back of his neck, as he moved over to the window.

Kari looked at Carla. "Are you okay?" she asked her.

"Yes, ma'am."

Kari wanted to tell her to take the rest of the day off, but that would only aid her case should she later decide to sue. "Get back to work."

"Yes, ma'am. And thank you, Miss Kari. I mean, Mrs. Drakos."

Kari smiled. "Get back to work."

"Yes, ma'am." Then she looked at Alex. "You told his arrogant ass, Mr. Drakos!" she said happily.

"Carla!" Kari deplored. Although Alex

didn't turn around, he smiled. And Kari smiled too. "Get back to work, child," she said.

Carla laughed. "Yes, ma'am," she said, and left.

Kari exhaled and plopped down behind her desk. "Two firings in a matter of minutes," she said. "That has to be a record."

Alex turned and sat on the windowsill. "Who else?"

"The head of Housekeeping."

"Oh." Alex didn't ask why. He really didn't care. "What did Bud do exactly?" he asked.

"He slapped the maid because she told off one of the high rollers who groped her."

"He slapped her?" Alex asked.

Kari nodded. "And wouldn't apologize either. He felt it was his right."

Alex shook his head. "He was becoming a problem anyway."

"What kind?"

"Harassment of the sexual nature. I've

heard some complaints. I was going to address it."

"Any lawsuits?"

"No. Thank God."

Kari looked at him. "How are you feeling today?"

"Tired of meetings after meetings and nothing gets done. We don't have enough information."

"How does it work?" Kari asked. "Have they physically moved into your office building?"

"No, and they won't. I owned that building before there was a Drakos Corporation."

"That's good. But you haven't met any of the players yet?"

"Not-a-one," said Alex. "But that's not the point Dimitri's making anyway. He wanted the company, but he also wanted to kill me, kill you, and to bring me to my knees. All three if he could get away with it."

"Some would say he did," Kari said. "At

least with the company."

"Some would say," said Alex, his eyes darting away from Kari's.

"Sharon, she's the housekeeping supervisor I fired, even she had the nerve to bring up that takeover as if we're on our way down anyway. It was pathetic."

"Is it?" Alex asked and began pacing the floor.

Kari could tell he was only half there. "What's the matter?" she asked him. "Other than everything, I mean?"

"Nothing," Alex said, "and, as you said, everything." Then he stopped in front of her desk, but he remained turned sideways to her. "The lawyers seem to think we don't have a legal leg to stand on. The takeover was above board. It was like a pickpocket in broad daylight and shame on us for the pickpocket. The fact that we were distracted and not paying attention doesn't make it wrong. Or illegal."

"But it makes you mad," Kari said.

"I'm angry as hell, Karena," Alex admitted. "The more I think about it, the angrier I get. I worked for decades building up that company, and he wants to take it from me just like that? And expect me to let him?"

"He expected you to be dead, which would have made the takeover easier," said Kari. "That was his calculation."

"But we thwarted those plans. Now I've got to figure out the rest."

"No word from Oz?"

"None."

"It'll happen. We've got to be patient, though."

"How can I be patient? The longer this takeover goes on, the more legitimacy it'll gain. It's the talk of the business world as it is. How Alex Drakos got snookered. How Alex Drakos went from being one of the richest men in America, to just another man. That was actually one of the headlines. Unbelievable."

"Just don't get caught up in it," said Kari.

"That's what he wants."

"I'm sure it is."

"But what I don't understand is the timing," Kari said. "Why now when what you did happened so long ago?"

Alex shook his head. "I have no answer for that myself. We checked prison records here and abroad, but Dimitri has been a free man. That's not it."

"Then what is it?"

"I couldn't tell you." Alex rubbed his neck again. "But something had to trigger it."

"That's what I'm saying. After all these years? Has to be something new going on."

But then there was a knock on the open door and Oz stepped in. "I figured this was where you were," he said.

But Kari and Alex both were looking at him.

"What have you found?" Alex asked.

Oz closed the door behind him. "I heard you've had an eventful day so far," he said to

Kari.

"You can call it that," she said.

"What have you got?" Alex anxiously asked.

Oz let out a sigh. "We've found him," he said.

Kari looked at Alex and stood up. Alex was staring at Oz. "Where?"

"You aren't gonna believe this."

"Just tell me. Where?"

"Right over In Pensacola. Literally less than thirty minutes away. He rented a house there like a month ago. Like that was his work shed. He's been there ever since."

"And our guys have him in view?" Alex asked.

"As we speak, yes. He's in plain view."

"Who's in that house with him?"

"Two of his goons, according to our guys. They saw him and his goons going in with a couple of gorgeous ladies. The ladies left, but he and his goons remained there. They're still there."

Then Oz had a blueprint rolled up in his arm. They hurried over to Kari's conference table. Kari went over there with them. "This is the layout of the house," Oz said. "Kind of simple layout, but there could be traps."

"What kind of traps?" Kari asked. "Boobytraps?"

"No. Hidden rooms. We just don't know. Because this is the original blueprints. There's no telling if he made any changes or additions. But this is the master bedroom. He may or may not be in there. But I called some of my people in Greece who used to know Dimitri. They said he usually slept in the smallest room in the house in case somebody broke in looking for him. All of the rooms are upstairs, so I would start here," Oz pointed out. "That's the smallest room in the house. I would begin there."

"Maybe we should ask the neighbors what they could tell us before Alex make any trips over there," Kari said.

But Alex and Oz both were shaking their heads. "That will only arouse unneeded suspicion," said Alex. "I know Dimitri. He's no dummy. He's a smart man. The element of surprise has to be on my side."

"That's why I had to pull the guys away," said Oz. "Once they eyeballed him, we had them waiting three blocks over in an upstairs warehouse view we commandeered. They can see who's coming and who's going from that residence by telescope. So it's not an ideal situation."

"They never are," Alex said as he took the blueprints and rolled them back up. "But I'll handle it."

"The best you'll be able to get is infrared viewing once you get inside," said Oz. "Body heat."

"It'll have to do," Alex said.

Kari didn't know what kind of infrared viewing they were talking about, but they knew what it meant and that was all that mattered to her.

"I'd better get myself prepared," said Alex as he began to head toward the exit.

"I'll go with you," Oz said, about to follow him.

But even Kari knew that wasn't going to fly. And it didn't. "You're staying right here," said Alex to his younger brother.

"But Glo called. She heard about the takeover and she's on her way back home. Her brother Teddy is bringing her on his plane. And you know Teddy's skills. He's Mick Sinatra's underboss so you know he's the ultimate protector. He'll stay with the family."

"But he's not here yet," said Alex, "and I'm leaving now. I don't want any lapses, Odysseus. You will stay with my family in case this house in Pensacola is another distraction and he's planning some of his shit right here at The Drakos. That's the only way you can help me. Guard my wife and my children."

Oz nodded. How could he argue with

sensibleness? "I will."

But Kari grabbed Alex and turned him to her. Because she knew her husband. "Remember the goal, Alex," she said to him. "Get your company back. And then get your revenge. In that order. Because if you lose that man, and he's not alive to rescind that takeover and hand you back your company, you may never get it back."

Alex nodded. He understood. And then he kissed Kari on the lips and stared at her a moment longer. And then he took off.

A look of desperation appeared on Kari's face as she watched her husband go it alone. Then tears. And then Oz was pulling her into his arms as she began to sob.

CHAPTER TWENTY-THREE

He parked a street over and jimmied the lock of a side door on the backside of the house. The door led to stairs and he slowly, carefully tiptoed his way up those stairs. He pulled out his small infrared camera and stuck a signal pod against the wall as he walked up the stairs. Although he couldn't see individuals on the camera, he could see the heat individuals generated on the camera. There was heat in the hallway, not outside the master bedroom, but outside the smallest bedroom upstairs. That would undoubtedly be one of Dimitri's bodyguards, or goons as Oz liked to call them.

Alex also saw heat inside that bedroom. One individual in a prone position. That would undoubtedly be Dimitri asleep in bed. And another individual sitting up near the person who was laying prone. That would undoubtedly be goon number two. Alex felt better. At least he knew how to attack the situation. At least he knew what he was up against.

He put the camera in his pocket and pulled out his loaded Glock. When he got to the top of the stairs, he immediately peeped around the corner. That was when he saw goon number one. And, to Alex's relief, he was fast asleep in a chair, the girlie magazine he had been reading dangling from his hand.

Alex began putting a silencer on his Glock as he slowly, methodically made his way toward the guard. But just as he was two feet away from the guard and was ready to put him in a chokehold that would put him to sleep, or, if he woke up, would take him out, a sudden, unexpected, alarm sounded. It was apparently set up near Dimitri's bedroom and Alex had apparently triggered it just by stepping on one of the floorboards near that room.

And then all hell broke loose!

The guard quickly woke up, saw Alex hurrying toward him, and began pulling out his own loaded gun. Alex was able to shoot the guard before the guard was able to draw his weapon.

But that was only the beginning of Alex's troubles. Because as soon as he neutralized that threat, he heard the sound of more than one person running up the front staircase representing an even greater threat. A threat he had to deal with before he could even think about dealing with Dimitri.

He grabbed the guard he had just shot and put him as a shield in front. Four guards appeared on the landing, and as soon as they appeared, Alex began firing.

But they were firing, too, and Alex had to fire, hold that guard against his body for protection, and attempt to open the door of that bedroom.

Only the door was locked. Alex had to back-kick that door in even as he was defending himself. He took out one guard, and then another guard, but two more had taken cover and were still shooting.

It was so intense, and the door would not give way, that Alex ran out of bullets. He then had to drop the Glock and grab the magnum he had in his back pocket. But the guards were advancing on him so fast that there was no time. He had no choice but to throw the guard that was his shield toward the other two guards running toward him.

But that slowed them only briefly. They threw that guard aside and continued firing. But Alex had kicked that bedroom door in with an even more desperate, Herculean kick and it gave way just as the bullets of those two guards ricocheted off of the door jamb and came within inches of hitting Alex.

But Alex knew another guard was in that room and he was firing in that room even as he slammed that door shut.

But nobody was in there. The bed was unmade but empty, and the chair where another guard had been seated was turned over, as if the guard jumped up in a hurry, grabbed Dimitri during the gun battle in the hall, and took off. Alex saw an open door that led down another stairwell. And just as the two guards busted into that bedroom door, Alex took off down that side stairwell too.

But not before stopping and waiting. And as soon as those two guards ran for that open door, too, and were about to run down those stairs, Alex surprised them by still being right there waiting. And he fired on them in rapid succession. He took them both out. And then Alex took off down those stairs.

He had to get Dimitri Kalashnik or he

would have risked his life in vain. He had to get Dimitri!

By the time Alex made it down those stairs and out of that door, he was at the back of the house. He saw, near the back end of the house, a guard put Dimitri inside a black SUV. But then he saw the backside of the vehicle open, as if somebody else had come out of the small guesthouse on the property and was getting in too. Could that have been Dimitri instead? Or could it be another guard? Which meant more firepower for Dimitri.

But Alex wasn't sure who that was that had gotten in with Dimitri and his guard and he didn't care. All he knew was that he had to stop Dimitri. He get away this time, he may never be able to capture him again. As the SUV started speeding off, Alex ran toward that SUV and attempted to shoot their tires out as he ran, to slow them down. But he wasn't able to get close enough to have a good enough shot, and the SUV was gone.

And Alex had no choice but to run to his car, jump in, and take off after them.

He momentarily couldn't find them, which invited panic of its own, until he saw the big, black SUV turn a corner nearly a half mile up the road and Alex had to floor his Lamborghini to catch up.

He caught up and found himself right behind the SUV. But his suspicion was right about another guard in that SUV because he leaned out of the window and began to fire an assault rifle at Alex's car.

Alex had to swerve and slow down to avoid those bullets. But he kept going. He wasn't about to lose Dimitri. But he never fired back. He wanted Dimitri alive. He *needed* Dimitri alive. And they continued to speed through the streets of Pensacola.

But not for long, Alex knew, because the guard driving the SUV kept making sharp turn after sharp turn. He handled it. Until he didn't. Until he made one turn too sharp and ended up on two wheels.

"*Nooo!*" Alex yelled and slammed the palm of his hand against the steering wheel when the SUV leaned on two wheels and then lost complete traction. It lifted up and dropped down rolling. Alex counted five rolls at least before it landed on its side, slid nearly fifty feet more, and then came to a complete stop.

Alex drove up near the SUV and jumped out of his Lamborghini. And with his Magnum drawn, he ran to the crash site. But he was already smelling gasoline. He knew he didn't hardly have any time at all.

He got on his knees to look inside. All of them were contorted inside, as if nobody had been wearing a seatbelt, and he couldn't make out who was whom. So he started pulling out bodies. He pulled out the guard, first, who had been the driver, but the guard was already dead.

And then the front of the SUV burst into flames.

"Help me."

He heard the voice, but he was shocked to hear it. Because it wasn't the voice of some man. It was the voice of a little girl!

Stunned, Alex looked inside the SUV and saw that there was indeed a girl on that third row along with a woman too. That second guard he thought he saw get in that SUV was a woman who had apparently been in that guesthouse with that child. He immediately began reaching for those two. He immediately wanted to get that little girl out of there.

But the SUV was already on fire, and the flames were coming fast and furious. Alex moved toward the middle row of seats and reached back there again. "Grab my hand!" he was yelling as the flames consumed the first row of seats. It was so hot in that SUV that Alex was sweating as if he had been doused in water. "Grab my hand!"

Both the woman and the little girl reached for his hand, to grab it, but his reach wasn't long enough. And they were trapped by mangled

226

metal. And then the SUV exploded again with an explosion that knocked Alex off of his feet and threw him backwards nearly fifteen feet away from that SUV.

He landed on his butt and was able to sit up just as the SUV rocked again with another explosion that engulfed it in flames from the front end to the back end, with no give in between.

Alex couldn't believe it. Not again! Not again! Not again, he continued to scream.

But it had happened again. Another explosion, this time not caused by a planted pipe bomb, but by his decision to chase after that SUV. Another explosion, and another innocent victim inside. Alex could not believe it.

But then he heard sirens in the distance. He knew his freedom would be in jeopardy if the cops found him on that scene. He was the one who had broken into Dimitri's house. He was the one who had chased that SUV. Dimitri was the one who had taken his company from him.

He had motive and he had opportunity. They would get him for more homicides than he could count and throw away the key.

Alex was devastated, but he came to his senses enough to get his ass up, get back into his lambo, and take off in the opposite direction of those sirens. He took off, but his heart was hammering. He took off, but he couldn't see the road for his own guilt.

CHAPTER TWENTY-FOUR

The penthouse was pin-drop quiet even though it was filled with bodies. Kari was there, and so was Jordan and Oz. Angie was fast asleep in the nursery.

While Alex was gone, Gloria had arrived with her big brother Teddy Sinatra. And they both were waiting too. Gloria sat beside Oz, and had her arm around him, although they still had issues to work out, and Teddy sat beside his kid sister. They were half-siblings, but they were thick as thieves. Teddy wasn't going anywhere until Gloria was alright. And Gloria wasn't going to be alright until Oz was. And Oz wasn't going to be alright until his brother was back home, safe and sound.

It would be several hours later, but Alex finally made it back to the penthouse. When he walked in, they all got on their feet. But when Kari saw him, and saw the anguish and distress on his face, her heart dropped through her shoe. "What happened?" she asked him. "Alex, are you okay?"

But Alex just stood there. He'd been driving around for hours after that wreck, and he could hardly verbalize how he truly felt. "I'm okay," he managed to say. But nobody believed him. Least of which Kari.

She, along with the rest of them, went over to Alex. She stood in front of him, placed her arms around him, and she looked up at him. "And Dimitri Kalashnik?" she asked.

Alex leaned his head back. "He's dead," he said.

"Damn!" said Oz. He knew that meant there would be no rescinding of the takeover. Their company was lost forever unless they were able to devise a takeover of their own. A near-impossible task.

"I chased him," Alex said as if he was still working it out in his head. "Why did I chase him?"

"What do you mean, brother?" asked Oz. "You chased him, I'm sure, to make sure you captured his ass."

"The SUV burst into flames," said Alex. "They couldn't make that sharp turn, and the SUV burst into flames."

They all stared at Alex. Why would he be reliving that?

Then he exhaled. "I tried to save her," he said. "I tried with all I had to save her." Then he frowned. "But I couldn't."

Everybody heard it, but it didn't make sense. "You tried to save who?" Kari asked him. "Who's *her*?"

Alex looked at Kari. "The little girl. And the woman. There was a little girl and a woman in that SUV."

The sound of shock echoed in that room. "Good Lord," Kari said out loud.

Jordan couldn't believe it either. *Not again*, he thought!

And Kari knew the devastation Alex had

to feel. "Come on," she said as she kept her arm around him and escorted him up the stairs and into their bedroom.

Everybody downstairs looked at one another. Gloria went over to Jordan and pulled him into her arms. But Oz got on the phone. There was a major fuck-up in their intel, and he wanted to know how it could have happened. How could there be a child in that house, and nobody knew about it?

But even after he screamed at his Security chief and ordered a review, he ended the call thinking about his brother. Jordan had told him about the incident all those years ago involving Dimitri and his wife and kids. And now it happened again? Dimitri and a woman and child who could be Dimitri's new wife and kid were killed in that SUV? Killed because Alex decided to give chase because Dimitri was getting away?

Oz looked up those stairs thinking about his brother. Alex could take a lot, and he had taken a lot down through the years. But a man, even an alpha male like Alex, could only take so much.

And then Oz's phone rang. Ready to cuss somebody out yet again, he answered quickly. But it wasn't his Security chief. This time it was downstairs.

"Somebody's here to see Mr. Drakos, sir," the front desk security guard said.

"Yeah? Who?" Oz asked. *The cops*, he wanted to ask.

"A Miss Catherine Drakos, sir," the front desk security guard said.

Oz shook his head. "Catherine?" he asked. "*What the fuck*?" he said out loud.

CHAPTER TWENTY-FIVE

Upstairs, Alex and Kari were seated together outside on the lounger, on the balcony off from their bedroom. It was a sunny day, and they both needed the fresh air. Kari was leaned against Alex, with her hand in his hand, and Alex was staring out at the darkness that surrounded them. He kept reliving what had happened in his head. He couldn't get out of his own head!

"This shit used to didn't bother me like this," he said to Kari. "But when I couldn't save them, I almost gave up. Something I'd never do. I even heard the sirens coming, and I knew they were going to take my ass to jail over this one. A little girl involved? I knew they were coming for me. And I nearly froze, Kari. I nearly . . ."

"But then you got your ass up and got out of there," Kari said. "Right?"

Alex nodded. "Right. But this shit used to didn't do this to me." Then he exhaled.

"Maybe I'm just getting old."

"Or maybe you're just getting more fearful, Alex. You have children who adore you now. And a wife who adores you too. You're more cautious now. More caring. More everything! It's not a bad thing."

"Oh, yes it is," said Alex. "I still have enemies, and they aren't more cautious and adoring. I cannot let my guard down or that'll be the death of the family that adores me. Of you and the kids," he added as he looked over at her. "It's not a good thing. Because the only time my enemies will behave and leave my family the hell alone is when I'm sleeping in my grave. Don't you ever forget that, Kari."

Kari snuggled closer against him.

But Alex was still staring at her. "You hear me? Don't you ever forget that."

Kari looked up at him. She heard him the first time. "I won't," she said, confused as to why he felt a need to repeat himself.

But he needed to repeat it in case he was

one day gone forever, and she needed to carry the family on. She was tough enough. He knew that. He knew she could handle it.

Then she exhaled. "Just rest, Alex. We'll worry about whatever we need to worry about tomorrow. Just get yourself some rest."

It was easier said than done, and they both knew it. But Alex did wrap his arm around Kari and closed his eyes. But he was a long way from sleep.

Especially when Oz entered the open door of their bedroom, looked for them, and then saw them out on the balcony. He went out there where they were.

Kari saw him first. "Oz?" she asked.

Alex opened his eyes and looked at his brother.

"We got company, Alexio," Oz said.

Alex hesitated. He saw that look on Oz's face. "Who?" he asked.

Oz exhaled. "Cate," he said.

Alex frowned. "Cate? Catherine? My

daughter? What does *she* want?"

Oz shook his head. "I don't know. But she's downstairs."

Kari looked at Alex. "We've got to see her," she said. "She may know something about what happened. Why else would she be here right at this moment, Alex?"

The next time Alex saw that daughter of his he planned to be calling the cops on her ass. Now he was the one who had to run away from the cops. He began getting up. "Let them bring her up," he ordered Oz.

But even Oz was hesitant. "Are you sure?"

"No. But Kari's right. Why else would she show up now unless she knows something?"

"Maybe she's trying to get back into your good graces," Oz said.

"She never was in my good graces," said Alex. "Bring her to me."

Oz exhaled, but he did what his brother

ordered.

Alex helped Kari on her feet. "I still can't imagine why she'd be here though," she said. "What in the world would she want?"

"I have absolutely no idea," said Alex. "But there's no sense speculating. Let's go see what she wants."

Catherine "Cate" Drakos, Alex's grown daughter from his first marriage, was already in the living room pacing the floor like a wounded animal. It was her father she wanted to see, and she wasn't going to rest until she saw him.

When she saw him walking down the staircase with Kari at his side, she stared at him. All she'd ever wanted was his love and affection. All she ever got was coldness and distance and everything but what she wanted from him. She knew the fact that she'd stolen millions from him didn't help. She knew the fact that she'd done even worse shit than that to him and his family didn't help either. But Cate Drakos had an amazing way to think about only what she wanted to think about.

And right now, it wasn't about what she did to Alex. It was about what Alex did to her!

And as soon as he walked into that living room, she pounced. "How could you?" she asked him with venom in her voice.

But even with the venom, Kari and Alex both realized there was more pain in her voice than anger. "How could I what?" Alex asked her.

Tears appeared in her eyes. Alex and Kari both saw how devastated she was. "I just got the call," she said. "They said it was you. They said you killed Dimitri Kalashnik and the baby too. They said you killed them both. How could you, Daddy? How could you? Mom always said you was the coldest man she'd ever met in her entire life. Jonathan used to say that about you too. Now I see what they meant!"

Now Alex was getting angry himself. "What are you talking about, Catherine? What have I supposedly done? I took out Dimitri.

Was he your lover now? I thought the Prime Minister was your cup of tea. Is that why you're so upset? Because of that scum Kalashnik?"

But Cate just stood there shaking her head and allowing even more tears to flow. She did not have the look of some drama queen, Kari thought. She was devastated.

And suddenly Kari had an awful thought. An awful thought! She could hardly bring herself to ask it, because she knew it would devastate Alex even more. But she had to ask it. "Was that little girl in that SUV Dimitri's daughter?" she asked her. "Was she you and Dimitri's daughter?"

Alex was shocked. He looked at Kari. Why would she even say such a horrific thing?

And Cate frowned. "No, you stupid bitch!" she yelled at Kari.

Alex angrily moved closer to her, ready to slap the shit out of her, and Oz moved closer too. But Kari held them both back. Cate's putdown meant nothing to her. She needed to know why she was there, and how it would impact Alex. "Then why are you here?" she asked Cate.

Even more tears appeared in Cate's eyes. And then she broke down into agonizing sobs.

Alex had never seen his daughter so distressed. "What is it?" he asked her. He hurried to her and lifted her chin up to his face. "What is it, Catherine? Who was the little girl?"

Cate looked him dead in the eyes. "My daughter," she said. "Your granddaughter!"

Alex's heart fell through his shoes. And so did Kari's. Oz and Jordan and Gloria and Teddy were astonished too. They all looked at Cate.

"His *granddaughter*?" Oz asked with shock in his voice. "What are you saying, child?"

"I'm saying that little girl in that SUV he chased down and caused to explode was my little girl. That's what I'm saying!"

"You never had a little girl," Oz said. "You

never had any children!"

"Yes, I did. And Daddy killed her!" Cate began hitting Alex with her balled up fist, even though it felt as if she was hitting a brick wall. "You killed her! You killed her!" she continued to cry out.

It was Teddy who pulled her away from Alex. The entire Drakos family was still too stunned to do anything. And they all were looking at Alex.

"That's not possible," Alex kept saying. But what he was really saying, they all knew, was *dear Lord, don't let it be possible*!

"She was Dimitri's trump card," Cate said through her sobs. "It was his opportunity to get back at you for what you did to Nadia and their two little girls. It was a chance for me to get back at you for how you fucked up my life, and Jonathan's life. We were good kids who only wanted their daddy's love. But you wouldn't give it to us, you bastard! And now my baby's gone!" She tried to break away from Teddy to hit Alex again, but Teddy was the most muscular man in a room filled with strong men. She wasn't going anywhere.

But Kari had to know how. "But how did Dimitri end up with your daughter if he wasn't her father?"

"I didn't do anything!" Cate said as if that guilt was kicking her too. "I just let him keep her at that house. She was safe there with her Nanny. And I trusted Dimitri. He was an enemy of my enemy and I was glad to help him take Dad down. I was glad to do it!" she boasted. "He said he'll keep the baby with him, and when the time was right, he'd tell Dad he had kidnapped her. And Dad would go ballistic. That's all we wanted. I wanted Dad to hurt the way he hurt us."

"But why now?" Kari asked.

"Dimitri had been trying for years to take over Dad's company. And I was right there with him, trying too. Because that company is the true love of his life, more than you and that four-eyed boy of yours and even that pie-face baby of yours will ever be!"

She settled back down. "But Dad was always one step ahead of us. He was always on his game. So Dimitri decided we needed to take him off his game. We needed to distract him, and man did we. It worked like a charm. We started doing a little finagling here, a little there, and then we did the big thing. The takeover. While his ass was in Brooklyn chasing Bridgette Venew, we stole his company! It was the perfect opportunity."

Then her tears returned. "But you had to go and kill Jovani. You had to go and kill my baby!" She burst into tears again.

Teddy held her, only because she was a grieving mother, but even he knew Alex's daughter was bad news.

And Alex was floored. Was it true? Had he really killed his own grandchild? A grandchild he didn't even know he had? Was it really true?!!!

And Alex couldn't take it. He stumbled backwards.

And then the big man fell.

CHAPTER TWENTY-SIX

The penthouse was as solemn as it was quiet. After checking out her story, and after confirming that she did indeed give birth to Jovani Drakos in Greece a year ago, Cate was taken to a safe house so that she wouldn't go blabbing to the police. But it also gave them time to see what Alex wanted to do next. Because he was in no condition right then and there to make any decisions.

Now he was in bed with Kari. She, and the rest of the house, had long since fallen asleep although it was still early in the evening. But Alex couldn't sleep a wink. He was still reeling from the news. Not only had his pursuit caused a child to be killed, but it was his own *granddaughter* that had been killed. His own grandchild!

He got out of bed. He had to think. He had to decide what his next move could possibly be. But first he had to get to that safe house to see his daughter. And to find out all he could about his granddaughter. The baby whose hands he had reached for, and she was reaching for him, when destruction came. He took out Dimitri's little girls and had no problem, back when it happened, calling them collateral damage. It was the good suffering because of what the bad had done. Now his own flesh and blood could be called the same. His grandbaby suffered for what he had done. Now he knew how Dimitri must have felt. Now he knew how all of those other victims of his collateral damage must have felt. And he was ashamed.

He looked over at Kari. She was sleeping so peacefully even though he knew she was in turmoil too. And he thought about poor Jordan. He didn't even look to see what effect the news had on Jordan. He was too busy reeling from the effect the news was having on him! But he knew Jordan was devastated too.

All because of him.

It was always all because of him.

He kissed Kari on the forehead, and then he eased out of bed. He dressed quickly, in the clothes he had several hours ago discarded, and he left the penthouse.

When he got out front, to where his Lamborghini was always parked, he saw, heading straight for The Drakos hotel, a line of what looked like six or more police cars. They didn't have their sirens on, which meant they didn't want to tip their hand, but he knew why they were coming. He also knew, if they took him in, they were never going to let him go. He knew, if he stayed there, he would be charged with the murder of all those bodyguards back at Dimitri's house, the three additional adults in that SUV, and his own granddaughter. The death penalty would be considered getting off easy for him.

There comes a time when fate steps in and decide your course of action for you. As Alex saw those police cars head his way, he just knew that was one of those times. And he let fate decide it. He was downstairs. He was at his car. Had he still been upstairs, he would have been in police custody within the hour. Dragging his family through a protracted lockup and trial and certain conviction.

But he wasn't upstairs. He was at his car. He had already, in fact, opened his car door. So he got in, and took off. When he saw the police cars give chase, and then turn on their sirens in case he had any doubt, he floored his sportscar.

And a local chase in Apple Valley became a three-state chase that ended on the Tallahatchie bridge in Money, Mississippi.

There was a roadblock of more than twenty police cars waiting for Alex on the apex of that bridge. But he never let up from the gas petal. He, in fact, floored it again when he approached them, causing many cops to panic and dive for their lives.

But Alex wasn't trying to hurt anybody else. He'd done enough damage for one lifetime. He swerved his car away from those cops, and then swerved toward the bridge rail. But he swerved so hard, and with such force that the car went airborne, missing the railing altogether, and ended up sailing high above the waters until he came crashing down. And his car tore through those waters like a missile hitting its target.

And it was a mighty target to hit.

Alex took on water immediately.

And then Alex Drakos went under too.

CHAPTER TWENTY-SEVEN

"Ma, it's on. Ma, it's on!"

Kari had just gotten off the phone with Vegas casino mogul and Alex's friend Reno Gabrini. He'd heard about the situation and wanted to know if there was anything he could do. She thanked him but told him his other family members, the Sinatras, were there. She had all the support she needed.

She was in the dining room surrounded by Gloria Sinatra and her father Mick Sinatra's wife Roz, and her uncle Big Daddy Sinatra's wife Jenay, and her brother's wife Nikki. Faye Church and Lucinda Mayes, Kari's closest friends, were also seated around that table comforting Kari after she was awakened by police and the harsh reality that Alex was no longer in bed beside her. According to the Police, and via video footage she later pulled up herself, Alex was heading to his car when the

Police were driving up to arrest him on multiple murder charges. *Multiple* murder charges, they said! Instead of allowing them to take him into custody, he sped away, forcing the Police to chase him.

Which was disturbing enough. Which was devastating enough. But now they had more news?

When Jordan ran into the dining room to tell them it was on, Kari and the ladies did not ask what was on. They assumed it had everything to do with Alex. They hurried to the living room.

Jordan, Oz, Teddy, and Faye's husband Benny were already there, along with Gloria and Teddy's father Mick Sinatra and Mick's big brother Big Daddy Sinatra. It took Mick and Big Daddy, along with their wives and Nikki, less than two hours to fly in from Philly and Maine on Mick's private jet. But Alex was still missing when they got there. But they all had come because Gloria had married a Drakos. The

Drakos family was now considered a apart of the Sinatra family.

They all were sitting down staring at the television set when Kari and the ladies hurried in. Oz and Jordan were on the edge of their seats.

"What is it?" Kari asked them.

"They're about to show ariel footage, Ma," Jordan said. "Of the chase."

Kari sat on the arm of the sofa where Mick, Oz, and Jordan were seated, while Roz sat beside Jordan, and Gloria sat on the floor between Oz's legs. Nikki sat on the arm of Teddy's chair, while Jenay sat on the arm of the chair where Big Daddy was seated. The only person missing was Angie, who was still asleep in her bed. Faye and Benny and Lucinda remained standing as they all stared at the television set waiting for that footage.

And finally it came. A live view from the news helicopter. As soon as Kari saw Mick's Lamborghini speeding through the streets of

NOTHING LEFT TO LOSE

various Mississippi towns, her heart squeezed in pain.

"It's been well over three hours," said the chopper reporter's voiceover, "with speeds at some point in excess of a hundred miles per hour, and then much slower speeds as Mr. Drakos continues to evade Police. Wanted for multiple murders and other felonies, he is a very desperate man taking the desperate way out. Because he has to know there's no way out this time."

Kari shook her head. She was praying he would be alright. Just surrender, she wanted to say, and let the lawyers handle it, but she knew surrendering wasn't in Alex's DNA. There was no way, she knew, he would ever surrender. Which gave her heart palpitations. Because the end seemed so inevitable.

And that chopper reporter kept on talking as they continued to broadcast the chase. "After his company was seized in a hostile takeover that left him reeling," the reporter said, "and with his fortune collapsing, it is the saddest chapter in the life of a famed New York businessman who became Florida's golden boy. The man who brought us The Drakos, the most luxurious hotel and casino we've ever had, and who put Apple Valley on the map as a tourist attraction that could someday rival Vegas. But now he's on the run. Now Alexander Drakos is a fugitive from justice."

There wasn't a dry eye in that room as they stared at the man they all loved and admired. Kari had tried to phone him on his cellphone, but he had left it at home. She tried several times to phone him on his car phone, but it only rang and rang and then would go to voice mail. Now she understood why. He couldn't look away from the road for a second, the way he was driving.

But then they saw the inevitable happen. A roadblock with what looked like two dozen police cars with sirens twirling and police officers with their rifles drawn and ready were waiting for Alex on a Mississippi bridge.

Everybody in that room leaned forward when the chopper pulled back and showed Alex's Lambo heading straight for that police roadblock on that bridge. They all held their collective breaths. Because it didn't look like Alex was slowing up for a second. Even police officers were diving to avoid what looked like a certain collision and shootout.

But then Alex's car swerved violently, as if he wasn't going to harm any of those cops. There were many gasps in the room because it appeared as if Alex had lost control of the vehicle and went across the lane, and then went airborne and sailed over the bridge. Most in that living room jumped to their feet with gasps and cries of pain and sorrow as the chopper showed Alex's car making a swift nosedive for the river.

When Kari saw that car swerve and then fly over the top of that bridge rail, she couldn't take it. "*Nooo!*" she cried as she began to slump down to her knees. "*Nooo!*"

Jordan and Oz quickly grabbed her, holding her up, but her body remained limp in a drooped down state. And she continued to stare at that TV.

And when Alex's Lambo fell through that water, Kari's heart fell too. It was as if she was watching a movie, not her own life. Not her own husband. Not the father of her children.

And Mick Sinatra, a man not ever known as a man of affection, hurriedly placed his arms around Kari's waist, lifted her up, and then pulled her into his arms. And Kari sobbed uncontrollably in his arms.

Then Mick looked at his wife Roz. "Call the doctor," he said to her, his own usually stoic face a mask of anguish too. Because he was fond of Drakos too. Because even he was worried about Kari. "Call the doctor."

CHAPTER TWENTY-EIGHT

Kari had been taken to her bed for nearly three hours and now had covers up to her waist as she sat with her back against the headboard in the middle of that bed. Jordan, with his baby sister asleep in his arms, was sitting in bed on one side of her, and Oz and Gloria were sitting on the other side of her. Mick and Roz, and Big Daddy and Jenay were also in the room, while Faye, Benny, and Lucinda, along with Teddy and Nikki, were still downstairs fielding phone calls from friends and business associates and making certain Kari was not disturbed at all.

Because she was disturbed enough. Everybody in that penthouse, and that bedroom were. It was as if they could not believe that awfulness was Alex's end. That was why they continued to watch news report after news report of that fateful chase and crash off that bridge despite the doctor insisting reliving it was

258

not a good idea. But it was Alex in that loop. *Their* Alex. There was no sweeping that kind of pain under any rugs.

But suddenly, just as Kari and those in her bedroom were watching more news reports showing the police running down to the river's bank knowing that kind of fall was not survivable, but shooting into the water just in case, something happened. Kari was startled. She saw Alex's face flash before her very eyes. He was in pain, and he looked anguished almost beyond recognition, but he was alive. He was alive!

Jordan, who had been taking peeps at his mother the whole time, saw her eyes go from staring seemingly unblinkingly at the television screen to eyes that were darting around the room like a wild woman, as if she was realizing something she had not even considered before. "Ma, what's wrong?" she asked him.

And suddenly Kari began kicking the covers off of her and getting out of bed, as if those covers were hampering her realization.

"Hold on there, Kari," Big Daddy said to her. "Take it easy."

But she was determined. "I've got to go get him," she said.

"Go get him?" asked Oz. "Kari, his body hasn't been recovered yet. The Police are gone for the night."

"We've got to find him," Kari said again, putting on her shoes.

Roz and Jenay glanced at each other in pure agony. They would be acting just like her had it been Mick or Big Daddy. And even they saw her hysterics as some sort of break with reality.

But Mick saw something different. "What did you see?" he asked her.

She looked at him. Did he see it too? "I saw Alex," she said to him. "He's not dead."

Jordan frowned. "Ma, don't!" he decried. "It's hard enough! He's gone. You have to face facts. We saw it with our own eyes. Daddy's dead!"

"He's not!" Kari insisted. "I'm not crazy. I saw Alex. We've got to find him before the police does because he's not dead. He needs me." Her voice sounded desperate, as if she was indeed having that reality break.

But she was insistent. "He's alive," she continued. "Alex would not have left me like this."

Oz frowned. "What are you saying? Karena? He had no choice. He was either going to be shot dead by those cops on that bridge, or killed by that raging river below and those thousands of rounds of bullets those cops were shooting at him even as he went into that river. He had no choice!"

"He's not dead!" Kari yelled back at Oz. "I would feel it if Alex wasn't walking this earth anymore. I would feel it!" Then she looked at Oz. "Take me to that river," she said.

"Kare," said Oz, with pity in his voice.

"I don't want your pity!" Kari proclaimed.

"Don't you dare pity me! Take me to that river or I'll take myself!"

Oz looked to Mick and Big Daddy for help. They were two of the most powerful men in America. Surely they could bring Kari back down from that ledge she'd plopped herself onto.

But neither man would ever question a wife's intuition. "Take her," Mick said.

"Take her," said Big Daddy.

Although neither man took any joy in their conclusion, and both seemed as distraught as Oz was, Oz still couldn't believe they would sign off on this wild goose chase.

"I'll go alone if I have to," said Kari, ready to leave. "But I'm going."

"Alright, alright!" Oz gave in. "I'll take you."

Maybe he needed that closure too. Because that was what this journey would be about. Closure. Not some rescue mission like Kari had in mind. And he knew Mick and Big

Daddy understood that too. It was for Kari's closure. It was so that the widow of Alex Drakos could feel in her heart that she'd done all that she could do.

But even after Oz ordered his pilot to get to the airfield, and even as Oz and Kari hurried out of the penthouse undetected by lingering press people, Oz still dreaded the mission. He didn't know if he could take looking at the very site where his beloved brother took his last breath on earth. And even worse, he didn't know if Kari could take it either.

But one thing he knew for sure was that closing a chapter on the life of a man like Alex Drakos was going to be impossible. It was a fool's mission all the way around.

CHAPTER TWENTY-NINE

She stood on that Mississippi bridge in the late-night air and saw nothing. The police had dragged the river until nightfall, uncovering nothing too, and now Kari felt nothing as she and Oz stood on the top of that bridge. There were two SUVs waiting: one carrying Kari and Oz. The other one their security detail. Just in case Kari wasn't some distraught widow seeing things, but was actually on to something. Oz normally had total faith in Kari's intuition, but he knew how love could blind you. He knew how the kind of love Kari had for Alex could be crippling when the fairytale was over.

And it looked as if his conclusion was right when they saw nothing and felt nothing. There was nothing there to see or feel. Until Kari had another request.

"Take me to the other side," she said.

Oz looked at her. "What other side?" he asked her.

"The other side of this river," Kari said, and hurried to get back into the SUV.

"Lord, my sister-in-law is gone crazy," Oz said as he shook his head. Why did Mick and Big Daddy go along with this nonsense? She would have listened to them had they put a stop to it. But he knew they were there now. She needed her closure. He was going to do whatever she wanted if it would later make her feel better about it. Or if not better, at least less guilty.

He got back into the SUV with her, and he ordered the driver to take them to the other side.

It wasn't a quick drive around. It took nearly twenty minutes to get on the other side. And when they did, it was an even darker, narrower road they had to travel down. But this time they were at the river's edge. They got out and stood on that edge.

You couldn't even see the bridge side of the river from where they stood. But once again, they saw nothing and felt nothing. They had to have the lights of the SUVs just to see each other.

Oz looked at Kari as she continued to look around. "Now you see, Karena? There's nothing here. As much as I wanted you to be right. As much as I wanted to find him, too, there's nothing to find. He's not here. He's gone, Kari. He's gone."

Oz had tears in his eyes. He knew Alex all his life. He'd loved him all his life. He wished to God what she believed had been true. But reality was a burden they had to bear, whether they wanted to bear it or not.

And Kari felt the agony of defeat too. She had been hoping and praying for the impossible. But Oz was right. There was nothing there.

But instead of leaving, Kari sat down. She sat at the river's edge. The security detail in the second SUV were standing on the outside of their vehicle, and they all began to hunch their shoulders when Kari sat down. What was wrong with this woman, they wondered. The man was dead. She needed to face facts. Oz needed to put his foot down and make her face facts!

But they were just wondering foolishness. Nobody put their foot down to Kari except Alex. Oz didn't order her to do anything, because he knew he couldn't. He sat down beside her.

Kari wished she could say she felt Alex's presence, but that would be a lie. She felt nothing of the sort. But for some strange reason, she did feel a need, an overwhelming need, to stay there. And they did. For nearly half an hour.

But it was from the higher elevation of that SUV did their driver see something. It was way off from where Oz and Kari were sitting, but he thought he saw something move in the night. He grabbed the flashlight and jumped out of the SUV, ready to yell for the security detail to blanket Oz and Kari. He ran down to where Oz and Kari were.

"Boss, boss!" he yelled as he ran.

Oz and Kari both looked up at him, and stood up when they saw the urgency on his face. "What is it?" Oz asked.

"Further downstream, in one of those crevices, I saw something move. Or somebody," he said.

Kari's heart began to pound. Oz's did too. "Where?" he asked.

The driver took the big flashlight and

shined it in the direction of where he saw something. Oz took the flashlight. "You wait here," he said. "Tell the guys to come with us."

The driver did as he was told and Oz and Kari, with their four-member security detail, hurried around the water's edge as they made their way around the river's side. They didn't see anything for quite some time, but they kept on looking and walking through the muddy trail. The security detail was shocked that Mrs. Drakos was going with them, but it was no shock to Oz. Kari was the boss. They didn't know it, but he did. And they kept on walking. And walking. And walking.

And that was when Kari saw something too. "Over there!" she proclaimed.

"Where?" Oz asked.

Kari took the flashlight from Oz and began to shine it where she was looking. And she took the lead, hurrying toward a crevice.

And that was when not only Kari, but everybody in their group saw it for themselves.

The driver wasn't wrong. Kari wasn't wrong. There was somebody there. Kari felt it was Alex even before it was confirmed. And even though she was running as fast as she could to get to the spot, with mud kicking up on her clothes, Oz outran her to the location. And when he got there, and saw his brother prone on his back, looking exhausted but very much alive, his heart leaped with joy. "Alex!" he cried. "Alex!"

Kari was already crying. She had faith even before it was confirmed. And she dropped to her knees as soon as she made it up to her husband.

Alex opened his exhausted eyes at the sound of Oz's voice, but he actually managed to smile when he saw Kari.

"How did you find me?" he started to ask her.

Kari was so relieved to see him that she could hardly contain her joy. But she did contain it. Because she knew, if they kept him there much longer, the cops could discover him too.

270

They'd celebrate when he was out of danger. "We've got to get you out of here, babe," she said. And then she couldn't contain herself. "Oh, baby!" she cried and kissed him and held him.

"I started to give up," Alex said, his voice heavy with exhaustion. "I knew it would be best for the family if I just gave up. But I thought about you, and about Jordan, and about my angel. And I weakened, Karena. I couldn't do it. I couldn't leave my family. I had to fight. And I fought for my life. I held on and I swam. No bullets touched me. And I made it to the side, and I rested and swam and rested and swam. And when I was clean out of sight of everybody and everything, I hoisted myself up, and fell out with sheer exhaustion. I couldn't leave my family."

Kari placed her hands on the sides of his handsome face. And she kissed him again. "Thank you," she said. "And no matter what storm comes, we'll stand in it together, you hear me, Alex Drakos? Together!"

But then Kari realized that storm could be approaching at any second if they weren't careful. And she got back down to business. And ordered the security detail to carry him out of there.

And they did as they were ordered. They happily carried their ultimate boss out of that muddy expanse, along the river's edge, all the way back up to the waiting SUVs. They put him in the first one. Kari and Oz got in that one while the security detail got back in the second one, with orders to notify no one, and both SUVs sped away.

But Kari knew there was one person she was going to notify immediately. "I'm going to call Jordan," she said happily to Oz. They both were seated on either side of Alex's prone body as she held his head in her lap and fed him water, small sip by small sip. "He's going to be so thrilled. Oh my goodness is that boy going to be so happy!"

But Oz stopped her. "No," he said.

Kari looked at him. "What do you mean no?"

"The authorities think Alexio's dead. We have to make them continue to think that. He's wanted for several murders, remember? We've got to strategize first."

Kari realized that Oz was absolutely right. "Where do we take him?" she asked him.

"To the safe house," Alex managed to say.

They both looked at him. "The safe house?"

"To Cate," said Alex. "That's where I was headed when the cops arrived to arrest me. I wanted to find out what my grandchild was like. And who was her father. And why would she have allowed that monster to take her."

Kari and Oz understood. "Then that's where we're going," Kari said. "To the safe house."

Because they had a lot to figure out. Like

how in the world were they going to hide a man like Alex Drakos? How were they going to prove his innocence when even he would confess he wasn't innocent? He did break into that house. He did kill those guards. He did give chase to that SUV that ended up in the death of all inside.

Including the grandbaby he now wanted to learn about.

But just as they arrived back in Apple Valley at that safe house on the outskirts of town, there was a new news report circulating on cable channels. And it was on the television set inside the safe house. One channel was giving the names of each and every one of the victims of what they were calling Alex's crime spree.

To their horror, not one of the victims named was Dimitri Kalashnik.

To their delight, not one of the victims named was their grandbaby Jovani.

They were stunned.

CHAPTER THIRTY

"Why am I being held like a criminal?" Cate Drakos asked angrily when she saw Oz come through that door. "I'm your niece. I'm Alex Drakos daughter! I'm no criminal!"

But then she saw her father, along with Kari, walk through that door. He looked rough. He still was nowhere near a hundred percent. But he was *alive*? "Dad?" The guards had allowed her to see the news of his accident and all the reports of his crimes too. He was surely dead. Was she seeing a ghost?

Even the two guards in the safe house were shocked. They stared at Alex as if they were seeing a ghost too.

"Untie her," Alex ordered the guards.

But even though he looked worse for wear, he was still large and in charge in their eyes. They quickly untied her.

But Alex had not softened his stance toward his daughter. "Try anything and I'll kick your ass," he warned her.

But Cate was still staring at him. She was still stunned that he could possibly have survived. "How?" she asked him.

"Alex?" said Oz. "Alex?"

"What is it?" Alex asked as he and Kari both looked at Oz. They saw that Oz was looking at the television set, at yet another news report on Alex's crimes and crashes. Oz hurried over, grabbed the remote, and turned up the volume just as the anchorwoman was saying the names.

". . . .and the Police Department have finally released the names of the victims of that horrific car crash in Pensacola after Alex Drakos allegedly broke into the victim's home and then took them on a highspeed chase." Pictures were shown of three people Alex, nor anybody else in that safe house, had ever seen before. "They are Jim Richardson. His wife Alma. And their little girl Beth."

Alex, Oz, and Kari had the same strange expression on their faces: *What?*

"I thought you were going after Dimitri Kalashnik," said Oz, looking oddly at his brother.

"I was," said Alex, just as shocked as everybody else.

"Then who the hell's Jim Richardson?" Oz asked.

But Kari was rejoicing. "It wasn't your granddaughter, Alex," she said to him. And it was only when she said it did Alex and Oz realize it too.

Kari turned to Cate. "It wasn't your daughter, Cate!" she said. "It wasn't Jovani."

And Cate, too, seemed to realize it when Kari said it to her. She was still reeling from seeing her father alive. And she began to smile as she looked at the television set again. As she looked at the photographs of a regular American family.

"It wasn't my daughter?" she asked Kari, as if she needed to hear her say it again.

Kari shook her head. "No. It wasn't her."

But Everybody was confused. "If it wasn't Dimitri Kalashnik," said Oz, "and it wasn't Cate's daughter, then where's Dimitri?"

"And where's my daughter?" Cate asked, suddenly with terror in her voice. "Dimitri said she would be in that house. His bodyguard called me and told me he took off with my daughter and her nanny and that Daddy chased them. He said they crashed. All of them crashed. Including my baby. But it wasn't true?"

There was no doubt to anybody in that safe house that Cate was genuinely confused too. And elated. But worried still just as they all were.

And then, as if on cue, Kari's cellphone began ringing. When she pulled it out and looked at the Caller ID, she was shocked. "It says Dimitri Kalashnik," she said.

Alex and Oz were shocked. "*What*?" asked Oz.

"He's on the phone right now?" asked Alex.

"Ask him what happened to my baby!" cried Cate.

Kari quickly pressed the Speaker button after she pressed the answer button. "Hello?"

"Finally he pays." The voice had a deep Russian accent.

"Who is this?" Kari asked, to get him to confirm.

"This is the man he thought he killed. But he didn't kill. Because I planned it that way. Because finally he pays for all the sins he has committed. He thought it was me. But I am too smart for Alexio. I am too smart for any man alive. And I always will be. That's how Nadia and I stole nearly forty million dollars right from under his arrogant nose. That's how I made sure all tracks led to that Pensacola home where I supposedly lived. I lived there, alright, for all of one hour. Just long enough for your surveillance people to see me arrive with two beautiful ladies on my arms. Then we, of course, killed those ladies and stuffed them in a wall in the basement. And then me and one of my bodyguards dressed in the same clothing those ladies had worn, of course we had them made to fit us. But it looked to your men as if I was done with them and the two ladies were simply leaving a john's house. Which is exactly what I wanted your men to believe. When I, of course, was one of those ladies. And they had no clue!" He laughed when he said that.

Kari was dying on that phone. She held on with both hands.

"And that Richardson family?" Dimitri continued. "They were innocents. I kidnapped them when I took over their house. They were being held against their will. That bodyguard got Jim Richardson out of that house when Alex showed up, and another one of my men got the wife and kid out of that guesthouse out back. Alex was chasing victims when he thought he was chasing me. He caused victims to die just like he caused my two little girls to die. And that is why," Dimitri finally said, "his little granddaughter will have to die too."

"What are you saying, Dimitri?" Cate cried out. "You can't harm Jovani. You said you wouldn't harm my baby!"

"I say a lot of things," said Dimitri. "You are the fool for believing me." And then he laughed again.

Alex snatched the phone from Kari. He was ready to give himself up to save that child. But Kari tried to wrestle it back, and Oz took it away from both of them. "You have my brother's grandchild?" Oz asked into the phone.

"Ah. Odysseus. Alex's baby brother. You don't know me, but I'd know that voice anywhere."

"Do you have his grandchild?" Oz asked again.

"Yes. I have little Cate. Or whatever her name is." He laughed. "The legacy of Alex Drakos will continue with more suffering. She was to be my backup plan in case your brother managed to get out of it alive like he always manages to do. But this time he did it to himself. And there was no getting out alive for him. So now, the little girl will be the icing on the cake. As soon as I hang up this phone."

"Dimitri, I beg you," Cate cried out loudly. "You can't!"

But Dimitri wasn't even listening to her. "When Alexio died, I felt as if we were even now. I stole his company, which will make me a billionaire, and he's dead too. A good tradeoff, I thought. We are even now. But when I kill his grandbaby, that will give me the victory. And that's what I want. A clean cut victory. Isn't it beautiful?"

Alex knew he had no choice. The only leverage he had was himself for his grandchild. This time he snatched the phone from Oz even

282

in his weakened state. "There's only one problem with your analysis, Kalashnik," Alex said. "I'm still alive."

They all could tell Dimitri was in shock. He didn't respond for several seconds. "What?"

"I'm still alive," Alex said.

"But . . ."

"You want me," Alex said, "you will have to trade me for that baby."

"What if their lying, Alex?" Kari cried. "What if there is no baby?"

Alex knew the risk, but he also knew his daughter. She was not acting. "What do you say, Dimitri? Make your decision and make it now. No more delays. Or you'll be right back where you started from."

There was another delay, but not nearly as long as the first one. "Okay," said Dimitri. "Come to me. I have the baby with me."

"Where are you?"

"I'm next door to Apple Valley. In Pensacola. I'm on my way to the house I have rented while I watched your turmoil."

He gave the address. "Give me two hours," he said, and then he ended the call.

Cate was staring at her father. Would he really give up his life for her daughter? She was astonished.

But Kari and Oz were concerned. "What if it's a trap, Alex?" asked Kari.

"Kari's right," said Oz. "He's probably taking those two hours to boobytrap that house."

"Oh, I'm certain that's exactly what he's doing," said Alex.

They all looked at him. "And you're going there anyway?" asked Oz.

But Alex was in deep thought. And then he decided on his course of action. "You did the research on Dimitri, right?" Alex asked his brother.

"Yes. Why?"

"Is his mother still alive?"

Oz thought about it and nodded. He remembered the report. "Yes. Why?"

"If my memory serves me correctly, she lives in Georgia. Isn't that right?"

Oz nodded. "Yes. *Why*?"

"We can be there, by plane, within the hour," said Alex.

"Georgia?" asked Cate. "But he said he was in Pensacola. He wants you at that house in Pensacola."

"I'm sure he does," said Alex. "Let's go," he said to Kari and Oz.

"But what about me?" Cate cried. "Daddy!"

Alex looked at the two guards. "Tie her back up. Keep her right here until you hear back from me." Then he added, understanding what he still may have to do: "Or my brother."

And then Alex, Oz, and Kari headed for the exit.

"Daddy?" Cate cried again.

But this time Alex turned around.

And Cate was resolute. "Bring my baby back to me," she begged.

Alex wanted to tell her that her ass should never have given that child over to Dimitri Kalashnik in the first place. But who was he to judge a parent? He didn't have some stellar record with Cate and Jonathan. Who was he to judge?

He, along with Kari and Oz, just left.

CHAPTER THIRTY-ONE

It was a small, quiet house on a small, quiet suburban street in Conyers, Georgia. Petati Kalashnik got out of her station wagon with two bags of groceries in her hands. She made her way to her front door just as an SUV drove up and Alex, Kari, and Oz got out quickly and hurried across the lawn. Even if Dimitri was inside and saw them, by Alex's calculation they would get to the mother before he could drag her inside and use her as the ultimate leverage. Because the one thing Alex knew about Dimitri: he was a mama's boy. He loved his mother.

But she was a very old lady, and she didn't even hear or see Alex and his crew coming her way until they were upon her. And she was at the front door.

Alex quickly covered her mouth while Kari and Oz blocked out any neighbor views.

Alex knew he more than likely had to

speak in Russian for the lady to understand him. So he did. "Open the door and don't say a word. You understand?" he spoke in Russian.

The woman looked back at Alex and nodded. And then she unlocked the door with her key, and walked on in.

And immediately they heard Dimitri's voice. And he was speaking in Russian too. "I sure hope you remembered to get my Seltzer this time," he started saying, but Alex, Kari, and Oz had entered the small living room where he sat in a recliner with a phone in his lap and a tv remote in his hand. Alex, he immediately noticed, had a gun to his mother's head.

Dimitri jumped out of that recliner as fast as he could move. He knew they would not kill him until they had that grandbaby, so he made a run for it.

"Stay with Kari!" Alex ordered Oz in case there was some trap, and he ran after Dimitri. This time he eyeballed the man, he didn't just have some infrared body heat detection. And he wasn't letting him get away this time.

This time Dimitri was going to not only give Alex back his company, but clear Alex's name. But first he had to get Dimitri and find out where he had Cate's baby.

But Dimitri was nobody's fool. That baby was the nail in the coffin for Alex. And he thought of it that way to the bitter end. Because Dimitri wasn't running to get away. He was running for revenge. He was running upstairs to the nursery, where the baby was in bed alone, and he grabbed the child, ran to the window and was about to toss her out with the kind of force nobody would survive.

But Alex, despite his still tired state, put on the afterburners running up those stairs after Dimitri. And as soon as he saw what Dimitri was about to do, Alex leaped across that room, grabbed Dimitri by the neck, and pulled him back.

But Dimitri still had the baby dangling out of the window, and she slipped from his hands just as Oz ran into that room too.

But Alex grabbed the baby just as she slipped from Dimitri's hands, and pulled her back to safety with such force that Alex and the baby fell backwards onto the bedroom floor. She was crying, but she was safe. And Oz hurried to detain Dimitri.

Kari and the old lady came into the room behind Oz. And Kari was thrilled by what she saw. Because Oz had possession of Dimitri. And Alex, for the first time ever, was holding his one and only grandchild in his big arms.

She was safe.

Dimitri was in their custody.

Alex looked up at Kari and let out a relieved smile. Because all was finally right with the world. And with them too.

EPILOGUE

They went to Disneyworld.

They needed the break and didn't hesitate to take it. Alex dropped everything and Kari did too. They made that decision after Dimitri admitted, on tape, that he had set up all of those killings, and that he had stolen Alex's company with the intention to defraud Alex. That tape served as all the evidence Alex needed. And the DA agreed. All charges against Alex were dismissed, and the Securities and Exchange Commission overturned Dimitri's hostile takeover and restored The Drakos Corporation to its rightful owner.

Dimitri Kalashnik was in jail awaiting trial, and Alex, Kari, Jordan, Angie, Oz, Gloria, and baby Jovani were on their way to Disneyworld.

It was the condition of Cate's release and ultimate forgiveness for all of her enormous past sins: that she would allow the grandparents to spend all the time they wanted to get to know their grandbaby. When Cate found out that Jovani was safe, and that Alex was the reason she survived it all, she gladly agreed. She even was hopeful for a relationship with her father too. But Alex knew his daughter. He still didn't trust her, and he still wasn't laying any bets on any real reunion. He tried that before and got burned. With Cate, it would have to be one day at a time.

But he had his family and his grandbaby. That was all that mattered to him.

"Dad?" Jordan said as he held his baby sister and they all lounged on Alex's plane for the quick trip to Orlando.

But Alex was too busy staring at the beautiful little girl he held in his arms. "What?" he asked Jordan without looking up. All they knew was that the baby's father was a black man, because it was obvious, but Cate would not say who. "Just somebody I knew," she said. "What difference does it make?"

It made a hell of a difference, and everybody knew it, but nobody argued with her. They were too thrilled to have Jovani in their lives.

"Dad?" Jordan said again.

Alex finally looked away from his grandbaby. "Yes, Jordan, what is it?" he asked.

"You have a baby of your own you know," Jordan said.

When he said that, everybody laughed. Because it was true. Alex was all-in with little Jovani.

"Tell him, Jordy," said Oz as he rubbed Gloria's ever-expanding belly. She would not be allowed to get on any rides. But she still wanted to go. She still wanted to be a part of the family finally getting back to happy times. "He's acting like Jo's the cat's meow and little Angie's yesterday news."

"That is so not true," Alex said with a smile on his face. "And my little angel knows it."

"What say you, Kari?" asked Oz. "You think my brother's overdoing it?"

But Kari had been crocheting a bib for little Jovani. She held it up for all to see. "Why would you say that?" she asked.

The bib had stitched on it: *Jovani, the cat's meow*.

When they saw what she had stitched on that bib, they all laughed. Including Alex. Including even little Angela, who was right around Jovani's age.

They understood it. They were just getting to know their grandbaby. Even Angela seemed to have understood it too. And they all continued to make light of it. Because that was what they had. Family, happiness, and finally that beautiful bright light at the end of their tunnel.

Visit

www.mallorymonroebooks.com

or

www.austinbrookpublishing.com

or

www.teresamcclainwatson.com

for more information on all titles.

ABOUT THE AUTHOR

Mallory Monroe, a pseudonym of award-winning, bestselling literary author Teresa McClain-Watson, has well over a hundred bestselling books under her name. They include MaeBelle Marie, the Alex Drakos Romantic Suspense series, the Oz Drakos series, the Reno Gabrini (Mob Boss) series, the Mick Sinatra series, the Sal Gabrini series, the Tommy Gabrini series, the Big Daddy Sinatra series, the Trevor Reese series, the Rags to Romance series, the Teddy Sinatra series, the Boone and Charly series, the Monk Paletti series, the President's Boyfriend series, and the President's Girlfriend/Dutch and Gina series. She has also worked as an executive editor for many years and as an investigator for three. Recently widowed, she has attended Florida State University, Florida A & M. University, the University of North Florida, and the University of Mississippi at Oxford Summer Law Institute. A law school dropout, she holds a Master's degree in history and education and credits God Almighty for ALL of her success.

Visit mallorymonroebooks.com or austinbrookpublishing.com

for updates and more information on all of her titles.

See also amazon.com/author/teresamcclainwatson.

Made in the USA
Middletown, DE
11 July 2021